A Time to Choose

Richard Parker

A
Time
to
Choose

A Story of Suspense

Harper & Row, Publishers
New York   Evanston
San Francisco   London

A Time to Choose
Copyright © 1973, 1974 by Richard Parker

All rights reserved. No part of this book may be used or reproduced
in any manner whatsoever without written permission except in the
case of brief quotations embodied in critical articles and reviews.
Printed in the United States of America. For information address
Harper & Row, Publishers, Inc., 10 East 53rd Street, New York, N.Y.
10022.

Library of Congress Catalog Card Number: 73–18708
Trade Standard Book Number: 06–024678–2
Harpercrest Standard Book Number: 06–024679–0

First Edition

A Time to Choose

73-159

One

Stephen watched his father's face, which wore a heavy, brooding expression. Stephen knew that look well; the whole family did. Mr. Conway hated making a decision.

"I'll be very careful," Stephen said.

"Yes, I'd expect you to be," said Mr. Conway.

The rest of the family, seated around the breakfast table, said nothing. Kate and Mrs. Conway were not interested; Margaret was, but she knew that any interference from her could only spoil Stephen's chances. Mrs. Conway gave each person around the table a sharp, observant look as if she were noting it all down somewhere. All she said, however, was:

"More tea, anyone?"

Mr. Conway passed his cup. Kate, eighteen, and a year older than Stephen, picked up a letter which she had read once but now began to read again. Margaret, two years younger than Stephen, suddenly made a snorting noise, pushed her chair back so the legs screamed on the tiles, and went noisily out of the room.

"What was all that about?" said Mr. Conway.

No one told him.

Margaret had stamped right out to the back of the house and across the lawn. As she approached the garage door she said aloud and in a furious voice, "What a song and dance about driving a stupid old car!"

She wrenched the double doors open and latched one back against the wall. As she was pushing a lump of stone around to hold the other, she heard Stephen coming out of the back door. He galloped across the lawn, raising his knees high in exaggerated triumph, jingling the car keys in the air, and grinning like a maniac.

"He might just as well have said yes in the first place," she said. "All that deep thought and careful consideration—honestly!"

"Well, you know what he's like." Now that he had the keys and official permission Stephen didn't care. He didn't understand what his sister was making so much fuss about. "He just doesn't like being rushed into things. And you didn't help much, steaming off like that."

He opened the car door and hesitated before climbing into the driver's seat. "Do you want to come?"

"Sally's coming around. I said I'd go swimming."

"Cheerio then."

"Mind the precious paint."

"I'll drive it like a hearse," Stephen said.

He drove slowly down the drive, past the breakfast-room window, with the greatest decorum, his hands on the steering wheel exactly at ten to two. He grinned to himself as the faces around the table swung white toward the window, but he did not turn his head. Only when he was a good mile from the house did he allow himself to relax, resting his right elbow through the open window, dropping his left hand to the bottom of the steering wheel, and driving in what he knew his father would have called a "thoroughly sloppy manner."

The official business for which he had borrowed the car was to collect props and costumes from school and take them to a village hall for a performance that evening. When Stephen reached school he saw that the school minibus and half a dozen cars were already lined up by the gym. Parked ostentatiously a few feet forward of the others was a sleek, low-slung Mercedes. An admiring group was clustered around it. Stephen swung out and parked at the far end of the line, out of sight behind the minibus. He walked back and joined the group.

He found himself standing next to Mary Silver, a thin, sharp-tongued girl with whom few managed to feel at ease.

"Who's the hero of the hour?" he muttered to her.

"Can't you guess?" She screwed her folded arms even more tightly against her ribby, unfeminine chest. "Who else but the unbearable Streeter."

The English master came to the door of the gym in his shirt sleeves. "When you've finished genuflecting," he said loudly, "we might make a start moving this stuff."

The group broke up, laughing, and followed the master back into the gym to start loading. About twenty

minutes later the minibus drew out. A short awkward-
ness followed. Obviously, many of the group wanted to
go in the Mercedes but tried to conceal the fact with a
great deal of animated conversation. Mary strode across
toward Stephen. She seemed to punch holes in the air
with her kneecaps as she walked.

"Do you mind if I come with you?" she said, opening
the door.

"Jump in."

As they drew out of the playground she glanced back
over her shoulder. "I wonder who will be awarded the
golden apple," she said.

"Don't you find it awfully hard to get on with people?" Stephen asked.

She gave this so much thought that Stephen wondered if she had decided not to answer. He rather wished
he hadn't asked.

"That suggests," she said slowly, "that getting on with
people is what I ought to be trying to do."

"Or," he said, "that you sometimes seem to enjoy
spreading tacks on all the roads."

"Enjoy? I certainly don't enjoy it. But I know what
you mean. The question is, why do I do it? I'll have to
think about that."

She appeared to be thinking about it for the next
twenty minutes, for they reached their destination without exchanging another word.

"Well, thanks," she said, jumping out as soon as they
stopped. "For the ride and for the advice."

"I didn't mean to be giving advice," said Stephen.

"That's the best sort," she said.

4

After the stuff had been carried into the hall the group began to disperse. Those who were going back to town went in the now empty minibus. Stephen considered what he would do with his freedom. He was tempted to take the car for a run on an open road somewhere, down to Folkestone perhaps. But his father was bound to look at the speedometer to see how far he had gone. It would be a pity to make a bad impression his first time out alone. He headed back the way he had come, feeling deflated.

A mile or so later it occurred to him that he had already done two sides of a triangle; it would be shorter, and more interesting, to take the smaller country lanes and trust to his sense of direction. He swung right at the next turning.

Although he knew the area in a rough-and-ready way he was not familiar with these narrow twisting lanes. Not many of them were signposted, and even when they were, the directions suggested merely alternative routes to the same villages. In a general sense Stephen knew that he had to cross, first of all, a line of low hills, and beyond that, a narrow winding river. He stopped to search the glove compartment for maps, but apart from an Esso London map there was nothing. He could have asked at one of the cottages, but he felt it was ridiculous to have to ask one's way less than a dozen miles from home.

For a long time he was driving along a road that went in what he was quite certain was the wrong direction. The sun was hidden in an overcast sky but it was somewhere on his right. On the left was thin, continuous woodland, mostly chestnut. Now and then there were open patches where the trees had been felled and it was possible to see that the land sloped up in that direction. It struck him that he must be going along just below the ridge that he had to cross.

"Any road to the left would do," he said aloud. But for another mile the wood remained unbroken.

When the turning did occur it was so narrow that he had passed it before realizing it was there. He braked hard and backed. The road was so narrow that he couldn't make up his mind for some minutes. There was no sign or notice of any sort, but it was properly sur-faced and had a used look. It certainly went in the di-rection he felt to be the right one. In the end he drove cautiously down it. The tips of straying brambles tapped the sides of the car and now and then a low branch swept across the top. There were no widened places for passing. However, it was definitely going uphill. He went on for nearly a mile, feeling more and more anxious every minute. He was already beginning to wish he had kept to the main roads.

Suddenly he reached an open space and a crossroad. All four corners were grassed. Heaps of dried grass and weeds had been raked up on each corner. There was no signpost. He stopped and switched off. A heavy silence dropped over the car like a wet cloth.

He found he had to make quite an effort to get out. The air was still heavy and damp. The clouds seemed to have thickened, and the gray, leaden light picked out the reds and browns of dead ferns and fungus so that they seemed like sulky embers.

Stephen shivered a little and walked forward to the junction. The two roads that went off to left and right

were hardly more than tracks, rutted deeply with trac-
tor tires, overgrown, winding back into the wood. The
road that continued forward was unsurfaced but gave
the appearance of being well used. He walked a little
way up. The land on either side was unfenced. The
chestnut woods had given way to scrub of gorse and
bramble with only an occasional birch or hazel.

But when he reached the first bend he could see that
the ridge was less than a quarter of a mile farther. A
clump of Scots pines stood clear against the heavy sky
and the road obviously went through between the two
largest trees. Stephen recognized the landmark; that
group of trees was visible from his bedroom window.
He ran back to the car.

A few minutes later he was approaching the group of
trees. He sat high behind the wheel as if to look over
the top of the ridge even before he reached it. The road
narrowed between the trees so that there was barely
room for the car to pass. On either side were sandy
walls a foot or so high; the tree roots came out of these
banks and formed a sinuous mesh across the track.
White wood showed where wheels had worn through
the outer bark.

He was going so slowly at this point that when the
car reached the tree roots it almost stalled on the slight
obstruction. Stephen jabbed his foot on the accelerator
and the car jumped forward. At the same instant a
flash of dazzling yellow sunlight and blue sky lit the
windshield. Blinded, he braked hard. The tires slid sideways on the tree roots, the car lurched at the bank, and
the engine stalled.

Rather shakily, Stephen got out and took a couple

7

of deep, uneven breaths. He went around behind the car to see what had happened. Fortunately, the sandy bank had prevented any serious damage. The back wheel had ended up against the wall of sand. The hubcap was dented where it had struck the bend of a root, but otherwise the car was unharmed.

He slowly released pressure on the hand brake and let the car edge back a couple of feet; then he looked in the trunk and found a screwdriver and a rubber mallet. He pried the hubcap off and found a place where tough springy grass was growing in sand. By holding the outside of the hubcap down on the grass and tapping the inside with the rubber mallet he managed to take the dent out. It left a semicircular mark, but with any luck it would not be noticed. He fitted the cap back on and returned the tools to the trunk. Then he walked to the top of the rise to see where the road led.

He had been quite right; this was the top of the ridge and below him lay the river. It was quite narrow, but wound in long, snaking coils backward and forward through almost waterlogged fields. At some places it had flooded and swollen out into small lakes. The lane sloped away down to the left immediately after passing the pine trees, joined a larger road at the bottom of the slope, and continued as far as a small stone bridge. All this was clearly visible from where he stood between the pines. He identified his own house and turned back to the car, reassured.

Before getting in he looked around at the sky, wondering about that flash of sunlight. The low clouds were heavy and unbroken, so indefinite in their shape that they seemed more like bulging loops of gray sailcloth. He could not understand how the sun could have broken through and been hidden again so completely. In the end he shrugged his shoulders and got in behind the wheel again.

This time, prepared for the tree roots, he stayed in the lowest gear. The car pulled slowly and evenly toward the top of the slope. The front wheels hit the roots but mounted them without stalling. Once again the windshield was momentarily lit by brilliant sunshine. Stephen stopped, more cautiously this time, and slowly inspected the surrounding countryside. The light could not have come from the sun, for the clouds were still unbroken. He wondered if it could be some sort of reflection from the stretches of water below; some sort of mirage perhaps. It was odd because there did not seem, in all the gray landscape, any point from which such light could have come.

He sat for a few minutes, thinking about it. Could it be something to do with the angle of the windshield as the car mounted the rise? He released the brake a little and let the car run back very slowly, an inch at a time. Again the light came and this time he quickly tightened his grip on the hand brake and held the car. He dropped his hands off the steering wheel and stared.

There was no doubt about it; the whole of the windshield was filled with brilliant sunshine. And not only the windshield but everything beyond it. The sky was a hard cloudless blue. And beneath the sky the whole forward landscape lay bathed in the light, shimmering as if under intense heat.

Stephen jumped out of the car and stared wildly around. It was in the nature of a trick; a persecution almost. He thrust his head across the hood in front of the windshield but there was no light anywhere. He was alone on a hilltop. He looked inside the car again and the light still shone. It was as if the windshield were being used as a projection screen. But there was no projector and nowhere that a projector could have been concealed.

He got in again and started the engine. He edged the car forward, no more than a few inches, and abruptly the scene vanished and the sullen river valley took its place. He let the car run back and the scene returned. He felt a shivering between his shoulder blades and had to make an effort to control himself. For a moment he was tempted to drive quickly on to get away from it. Then the temptation passed. He closed his eyes and breathed deeply half a dozen times, calming himself and getting control. Then he opened his eyes and began to study the sunlit landscape carefully, detail by detail.

Two

At first Stephen could not help thinking of it as a picture, framed as it was by the car windshield. The sunlit landscape contrasted so abruptly with the car fittings and the surrounding gloom of the real day that it had only the pretended reality of something shown on television.

The picture was broadly similar to real landscape. The slope that fell away just in front, the river in its flattened valley, and the slow rise beyond. But on top of that, as if the countryside had dressed itself in fancy dress, was something more foreign. The colors were harder and brighter, the trees lacked the variety of English trees and were a duller green—almost as if they had been coated with a fine gray dust. The heat was foreign; not that he could feel it, but the sinuous movement and distortion of the distance, the glare from the yellow rocks, gave an unmistakable impression of heat.

At the bottom of the valley where the real river wound

its involved course, the strange picture landscape had an elaborate arrangement of oblong pools separated by concrete walls and paths. There were small concrete buildings, windowless cuboids, which could have been pumping stations or water control points. Men were working around the pools. The distance was too great to see exactly what was going on, but Stephen guessed that some sort of fish farming was involved.

Suddenly he became aware of a girl, seated on an outcrop of the yellow rock not very far in front of the car. She had her back to him and seemed to be watching the footpath below her as if waiting for someone. She wore a short, sleeveless, blue tunic that left her long, bronzed arms and legs bare. She seemed to be enjoying the hot sun. Every now and again she leaned her head back and gave it a little shake so that her hair, which was long and dark, hung in one straight fall to the yellow rock behind her, just touching it.

Although he could see only the curve of her left cheek Stephen felt there was something disturbingly familiar about this girl. Not familiar in the sense that he might have seen her serving in a shop or walking in the streets, but familar in a more remote part of his mind. She seemed to belong to some part of his experience less well documented than everyday life; from farther back perhaps, or even from a dream. There was certainly a dream quality about the scenery.

He moved his head to the left, trying to see more of the girl's features, and as he did so he realized at once that the scene in front of him had real depth. When he moved his head the near objects shifted position in relation to those farther away. At the discovery of simple fact the hair at the back of his neck prickle had really thought of the picture on the windshi a clever technical trick, but a two-dimensional trick a projected film.

In that second of discomfort he reached for the ignition switch, his instinct being to escape. But the sight of the dashboard and his own hands in relation to it gave him his own measure of reality, which had nothing to do with what seemed to be happening out there. If he opened the car door it would all disappear. It had its own reality perhaps, but he was no part of it. The act of driving away or getting out of the car would release him.

He had his hand on the door handle as if about to prove this to himself when the girl suddenly swung around, rather as if she had been called, and faced him with a look of obvious pleasure. She seemed to be looking, not at him, but at someone only a little distance to his right. Stephen turned his head to see who it was, but of course the view through the side window was part of his world; the gray overcast day and the scaly trunks of the pine trees. There was no bright sunshine or waiting friend.

The girl got up and came toward the car. She was certainly beautiful, with small, rather exact features and large green eyes. She was speaking to the unseen friend and laughing, with the pleasure of seeing him perhaps. Again Stephen had a vague feeling of familiarity, and at the same time a painful sensation of disapproval, almost as if he were jealous. He was puzzling over this when she passed out of his sight off the edge of the windshield.

For a few seconds Stephen leaned forward on the steering wheel, gazing vaguely down into the valley. Blue-clad figures were moving around the fish tanks, if they were fish tanks, making a pattern of sunlit activity. But he was not concentrating on this. He was trying to remember where he had seen the girl before, or if in fact he had.

He was disturbed out of this by a sudden draft of cold air, almost as if someone had opened the back door of the car. He even swung around to see, but all the doors and windows were shut and the lane behind was quite empty.

And then a voice spoke, quite clearly but somehow purified, as if it had passed through a filter. He heard nothing and yet the voice was there, a girl's voice, inside his head.

"It's cool in here," she said. "Come inside a minute. I've got something to tell you."

"All right," said a different voice, a boy's this time. "But only a few minutes. I'm on water control this afternoon and the flow stabilizers aren't working properly. I have to check every ten minutes or so."

And then there were two people inside the car with him, warm and breathing and, for the next few moments, silent. Stephen knew somehow that they were embracing. But where were they? As far as he could see the car was empty, but his head seemed full of them and the warmth of their affection for each other. He felt himself protesting at the trespass.

14

"What was that?" said the girl quickly.

"I didn't hear anything."

"There's someone in here with us."

The boy laughed. "You can see there isn't. There's hardly room."

"But I felt . . ."

"What?"

"I don't know. Something."

Stephen felt embarrassed; as if he'd been caught staring into someone's window. He opened the car door and climbed out as quietly as he could. Then he pushed the door almost shut and climbed up the bank to stand among the pine trees. As soon as he was away from the car he felt that the whole thing was ridiculous. How could there be two people inside his head? It was unthinkable. And evicting him, in the bargain. How daft can you get?

Even so, he didn't return immediately to the car; he sat down on one of the tree roots and leaned his back against the trunk. When he began to think of it he realized that he often had people in his head. It was a strange way of putting it, but true nevertheless. When he remembered incidents, the things people had said and done, there they were quite as clear as that girl on the hilltop. Well, almost as clear. When you thought of people, you could never inspect them or get them into sharp focus. There was a quality of blurring in the people you thought of. You could never improve on the observations you made at the time. If you had not noticed some feature you couldn't discover it by inspecting your memory. So there was a difference.

On the other hand, in dreams there was often more looking than speaking. When he compared the two experiences he saw that this vision through the windshield was more like a dream than anything else. A hallucination, a waking dream, why not? The longer he sat outside the car under the pine trees the more he was convinced. And what's more, he thought, quite excited at the idea, there is a very simple way of checking. Things that happened in your head waited for you. They didn't go on in your absence. You always picked up where you'd left off. All he had to do was to go back into the car. In any case it was rather stupid, sitting out here as if to avoid intruding. How could you intrude on your own thoughts?

He got up immediately and, feeling rather self-conscious, went back to the car. He opened the door and looked into the back and then slowly put head and shoulders through the doorway as if testing it out by degrees. He felt immediately that the couple had gone; the tension had relaxed and the car was its normal uncharged self. So the whole thing was over. Consciousness dispels illusions.

But when he swung around in the seat to face the front, the sunlit valley was still there and the blue-clad couple were only a few paces away, walking hand in hand and deep in conversation. The boy was saying something with great emphasis. The girl looked at the ground as she walked, shaking her head from time to time as if stubbornly disagreeing. They reached the rock where the girl had been sitting, went on down a track of some sort, withdrawing from his sight.

Stephen sat for some minutes trying to sort out his ideas. For some reason the stupid phrase "Back to the drawing board" kept recurring and interfering with any attempt at logical thought. However, he thought ruefully, if that meant his original ideas about dreams and hallucinations were clearly wrong, he had to admit the phrase made a sort of ironic sense.

At this point he was startled by a raucous blast of a car horn and turned to see a Land Rover on the lane behind. The driver was grinning, no doubt at the way Stephen jumped.

"Do you want a push?" he bellowed.

Stephen opened the door and leaned out. "Sorry," he shouted. "Didn't see you were there. I was admiring the view."

The driver of the Land Rover seemed to find this even funnier, for he threw back his head and rocked about with laughter.

Stephen started the car and let it crawl forward. The moment it moved, the scene in the windshield changed. The lane down the hill was narrow and twisting, deeply engraved in the sandy soil. He drove with care and concentration. He had crossed the bridge to the main road on the far side of the river.

As he turned up the hill he was already finding it hard to believe that anything out of the ordinary had happened to him. There was an inconsequential vagueness about the whole episode that seemed to put it more in the world of dreams than in the waking world of reality. He had driven to the top of the hill, skidded, and dented a hubcap. Worried about it, he had fallen into a doze from which he had been roused by a man in a Land Rover.

The explanation did not satisfy him. Had he in fact dented the hubcap?

The first thing he did after putting the car away was to inspect the hubcap. The faint, semicircular ridge showed where he had pushed out the dent; so that part at least had happened.

"You took your time," Margaret said. "We didn't know whether to wait lunch for you or not."

"You know what it's like," he said. "Anything to do with the Dramatic Club is always thoroughly disorganized."

"Not too disorganized, I hope," said Mr. Conway.

Margaret caught her brother's eye.

"Not to the point where it involved the car," Stephen said with a grin. "Streeter made a dramatic appearance with a new Mercedes."

"Streeter," said Margaret. "Yuk!"

During the meal Stephen said, "Will it be all right to ferry the stuff back tomorrow? They want to have it cleared by eleven because of Sunday School or something."

"Um," said Mr. Conway.

Margaret called this his "computer working signal." Stephen thought it was more like the "Wait" sign outside the headmaster's door. Conway himself knew that his children found his deliberations comic, but he also knew that it was far from easy to abdicate. Wanting to was not enough; other people's preconceptions had you hog-tied.

"I see no reason why not," he said.

He saw Margaret glance at her watch and give her brother a faintly amazed glance. Later, they would laugh together over his breaking some record or other in coming to a decision. He sighed fairly unobtrusively and asked his wife what plans she had for shopping after lunch.

Traditionally Stephen and his father washed up at Saturday lunchtime. "I'll wash," Stephen said and began to fill the sink.

They worked together in silence for a while. Stephen was considering telling his father about the morning's experience but could think of no way of doing so without getting involved in a tedious inquiry into his reasons for being on that particular lane in the first place. He could not dismiss the subject from his mind, however, so after a while he said:

"Do you know anything about space-time theories?"

"I've read a few bits and pieces. I shouldn't like to claim I understood it very well. Why? What's the problem?"

"Not so much a problem," Stephen said, "as a question of possibilities. Is it theoretically possible for two different things to occupy the same space at the same time?"

"Things?"

"Well, sets of things. Take this kitchen, for instance. And us washing up. Is it possible for another group of people, doing something completely different, to do it in the same space that we're occupying? In another dimension or something?"

Conway went on polishing the same plate for a long time. "You really ought to ask that math chap you've got at school—Wiggs, isn't it?—he's something of an amateur astronomer, I understand. Right up his street."

"I might ask him," Stephen said.

They continued in silence for a while.

"All the same," Conway said, "it's a fascinating idea. The way I've understood the theory, it's not impossible. I remember someone comparing it to one of those coaxial telephone cables. They can carry two hundred telephone conversations at the same time, each one inaudible to the others."

"Not impossible?" said Stephen. "In other words, possible?"

"There is a distinction. Probably in the matter of proof or disproof. And of course, whether such a situation is even remotely probable is another matter altogether. What started you off on the idea, anyway?"

"Oh, I don't know," said Stephen vaguely. He had decided to share his morning's adventure with no one just yet. Certainly not until it had been repeated. If it ever was. He wiped the sink out and wrung the cloth. "Well, that's that," he said.

Three

The school minibus had been packed with most of the stuff and had gone. Mary Silver sat on a costume basket, reading. Her legs, in blue trousers, were folded up in a half-lotus.

"One side will make you grow taller," said Stephen from the door, "and the other side will make you grow shorter."

"One side of what?"

"Of the mushroom."

"What mushroom?"

"I just thought you looked like the caterpillar in *Alice*."

"Sorry," Mary said. She lifted her foot with both hands, straightened her legs slowly, and stood up stretching. "My childhood mythology was *Winnie-the-Pooh*."

"God bless Nanny."

"Exactly. Which probably accounts for much."

The hall was cold and empty, and gave their voices an unnatural resonance.

"All this has got to go. Can you get it in?"

"No," Stephen said.

"You're a great help."

"At least I turned up. What happened to the others?"

She shrugged. "It is Sunday."

"They can't all have gone to church. Streeter?"

"Streeter phoned to say his father had turned nasty."

Stephen started to laugh and after a moment she joined him. The echoing hall seemed to enjoy the joke, shaking its sides like an amiable giant, ho ho ho. They carried out two baskets and some odds and ends.

"Someone will have to come back," Mary said. "If the Sunday School gets loose among this lot . . ."

"I don't mind. We never have lunch till past two on Sunday."

"We never have lunch on Sunday," Mary said. "We have dinner."

"I know all about your gruesome proletarian origins. I can't help it if my father's a schoolteacher." He opened the car door. "Are you coming, or staying here on guard?"

"Coming."

They took the baskets to school and unloaded them. As they started on the return journey Stephen said:

"You don't mind if we make a little detour? I found this odd lane over the hills yesterday."

"What's so special about it?"

"Perhaps you'll see when we get there."

He drove around so as to approach the hill from the river. Perhaps it can't happen this way, he suddenly thought. Like a one-way mirror. When they came into the narrow sunken lane he felt himself beginning to sweat. Mary Silver was hugging her knees. Out of the corner of his eye he thought she was moving her shoulders in an odd way. Glancing quickly, he saw she was laughing.

"What's bitten you?"

"This old lane you've discovered."

"So what?"

She pointed to a bleak little yellow brick cottage standing on the bank a little way ahead. "I was born in that house. Lived there till I was eleven."

"That's odd."

"It was cramped and squalid. Nothing odd about that."

"Skip it."

They were coming up to the top. He slowed right down as the car reached the clump of trees, stopped at the first of the tree roots across the road, and changed into low gear.

"Crossbills nested up in those pines one year."

"Crossbills!" He didn't believe her.

"I tried to climb to one of the nests and fell out of the tree. Broke my leg." She pointed at the road a few yards in front of the car. "Just there."

Stephen edged the car forward, watching the windshield and through it, the sky. As the front wheels dropped down after the last root there was a sharp sound and the windshield cracked in all directions.

Mary made a sharp gasping sound and then laughed. "Must be a jinx on the place," she said. "We're exactly over the place I broke my leg."

Stephen was not listening. He was puzzled. Through the cracked windshield the scene had remained unchanged. No sunshine. No tropical vegetation. Just the sandy, scrubby area on either side, leading down to the crossroads.

He moved the car forward a few inches at a time, keeping his eye on the edge of the road through one clear corner of the glass. The cracks remained. Nothing else happened.

"You can't drive with the windshield like that," Mary protested. She slipped a shoe off and held it by the toe so as to bang the heel on the glass.

"Wait!"

He stopped the car and fetched the rubber mallet from the trunk. He swung at the windshield but it was tougher than it looked; the mallet bounced off. He put a lot more force into the next blow and the whole of the glass shattered inward. Mary got out and started to shake the fragments out of her clothes.

"That was brilliant," she said.

"I should have done it from inside."

"You're so right."

"Sorry. Hang on, though! You're bleeding."

Mary held her arm up and looked at the blood dripping from a cut near her wrist. "Hell," she said. "It's on my clothes. Once it's dried on, you never get the stain out."

"I'll run you home," Stephen said. "It's all my stupid fault."

Mary hesitated. "No, look," she said, "I'll run down to Gran's house. By the time you've cleared that glass up I'll be back again." She went off without giving him time to argue.

Stephen opened both the car doors and began to throw out the larger pieces of glass. After about five minutes he realized that he would never get the smaller pieces and the dust cleared up without a brush. He decided to back the car down to the cottage to see if he could borrow something from Mary's grandmother.

The cottage was small, one of the sort built in the nineteenth century for farm workers, the front door opening straight into the sitting room, with two rooms downstairs and two up, no bathroom, outside toilet. The front door looked as if it hadn't been opened for generations. Stephen went self-consciously around to the back door, which he found half open.

"Mary!" he called. "Are you there?"

No sound came from the kitchen. From where he was standing he could see half of an old pine table, worn and scrubbed until the knots stood higher than the rest of the surface, and beyond that a dresser, and beside the dresser a wooden rocking chair with a red felt pad on the seat. It was more like a TV set than a real kitchen.

He tapped on the half-open door and then, still hearing no sound, slowly pushed his head inside. Mary was standing by the sink in an arrested pose with a wet dishcloth in one hand. She was looking straight at him as if she had been waiting for the moment when he would appear.

"What the . . ." he began.

She raised a hand sharply and made a face, telling

25

Central Jr. High School Library.

him clearly enough to be quiet. Stephen had no idea what he was supposed to be listening for. He leaned on the door and watched with a tolerant expression for what seemed a long time; two or three minutes at least. Then, as she still had not moved, he crept across and sat down in the rocking chair. The silence stretched on and on. He occupied himself with a more thorough inspection of the kitchen.

Abruptly Mary squeezed out the dishcloth and hung it on the tap. "They've gone," she said.

"Who've gone?"

"I don't know. It's . . . you won't believe me if I tell you."

"I could try. Sometimes I can believe as many as six impossible things before breakfast."

Mary managed to look both mystified and suspicious at the same time.

"Sorry. Wrong mythology. That's from *Alice* again."

"Well," Mary said after a moment's consideration, "I thought I heard two people talking."

"You thought?" Stephen felt a cold tingling somewhere between his shoulder blades.

"The voices seemed more inside my head than outside."

"Vocalized thoughts?"

"No. They were arguing. A boy and a girl. I didn't recognize the voices, although . . ." She hesitated. "The boy's voice was something like yours."

Stephen said, "Yesterday, an odd thing happened to me, rather like that."

"Is that why you came around this way?"

"Yes. It happened at the top of the hill. Just where the windshield shattered."

Mary thought about this. "There must be a trick acoustic somewhere on this side of the hill. I remember once on the South Downs I heard two people talking quite clearly, and yet I could see they were nearly a mile away. The curve of the ground or something. Don't they use a special shape for catching sounds? A parabolic reflector, isn't it? Maybe sometimes the land makes a natural parabola."

"In my case I saw something as well," Stephen said. "Perhaps . . ." He stopped and began to prowl around the kitchen, looking out of each of the windows to check on the view.

"Now what are you doing?"

"I thought it might have happened here too."

He stopped by a small door to the right of the fireplace. "What's in there?"

"It's just a cupboard. When the fireplace was blocked up part of it was made into a cupboard."

"There's a crack of light coming from it."

"There can't be. There's no light inside. It's only a tiny cupboard. Open it and see."

Stephen pulled the door open and bright yellow light spilled out into the dim little kitchen, dazzling them both.

"What on earth . . . !" Mary exclaimed.

Stephen however immediately recognized the scene. The aperture was a good deal smaller, being only the space between two shelves in the cupboard, and the view was partly blocked by a pile of tattered cookbooks and an old wooden tea caddy that occupied some of the space. Nevertheless, the bright hot sunlight and the vegetation, the dusty dried-out look of the pathway, and the patches of yellow rock told him that he was looking into the same world he had seen through the car windshield on the previous day.

This time there were no figures in the landscape. The hanging gray-green leaves of a tree moved slightly, swaying in an eddy of wind. A brightly colored bird flew up suddenly from the pathway and disappeared, and a moment later the picture itself began to dim and blur. The shapes ran into each other, darkened, solidified, and with a smooth transition changed into the darkened plaster at the back of the cupboard.

"That was it," Stephen said excitedly. "That's what I saw, only last time it lasted a lot longer."

Mary put her hand through to the back of the cupboard and pressed her fingers against it, testing the solidity. "How fantastic!" she said. "It looked almost real."

"I think it is real. Yesterday, I saw people, two of them quite close. They could have been the same two you heard."

"But I didn't exactly hear . . ."

"Tell me what they were saying."

"It's not easy to remember exactly. I didn't understand half of it. They were arguing about something the girl was going to do and they used words I'd never heard before, so I couldn't be sure what they meant."

"Well, roughly."

"Very roughly, I'm afraid. You know what it's like

hearing the middle of a conversation. Well, the girl, her name seemed to be Bitta or Vitta or something like that, not a name I've ever heard before, she'd been chosen for some sort of training and was all worked up about it. But the boy was dead against it. He kept saying he wouldn't see her for five years, and anyway once she'd become a sike she wouldn't be interested in him any longer."

"A sike? What's that, for pity's sake?"

"I don't know. But it seemed to have sort of medical overtones. She said something about healing powers. Oh, and she got very intense about if you were the one person in a thousand with natural psi-factor potential it was your duty to develop it for the good of humanity."

"What do you think she meant?"

"How do I know? You wanted to hear what they were talking about and I'm trying to tell you. I said I didn't understand much of it. The point seemed to be that they were quarreling about it and this boy—she called him Curwen—was trying to stop her going off to some college or other. She seemed pretty determined to go. And then they sort of walked out, still arguing."

"Walked out of where?"

"Wherever they were. Out of my head anyway."

"It must have been the same couple," Stephen said. "When I heard them the girl was saying she had something to tell him. And later on, I saw them walking away."

"We're talking as if they were real people."

"They must exist somewhere. We both heard them."

"Some sort of haunting, do you think? The spirits of

unhappy lovers coming back to the place they last met. Perhaps it all happened years and years ago."

"Sikes and psi-factors?"

"Yes, that was odd. Still, I could ask Gran if she's ever heard anything about such characters. She knows all the local legends."

"Where is she?"

"I don't know. Shopping, I expect."

They went out to the car and brushed out the fragments of glass. They very quickly agreed that someone else would have to fetch the remainder of the Dramatic Club's material, and Stephen took Mary home.

As he drove slowly back toward his own house he wondered why he had said nothing to Mary about the girl's appearance. Bitta, she said the name was. An odd name, but somehow it seemed to fit. Why, he wondered, was he so disturbed about her? He certainly didn't feel she was a ghost out of the past. She seemed very alive and real. Even at this moment, as he thought about her, he had a very clear picture of her sitting on the rock and turning to face him.

And then he knew for certain where he had seen her before. She was a figure in a dream he used to have.

Years ago now. He must have been thirteen or fourteen at the time. This girl, or one remarkably like her, had turned up night after night; a rather remote, romantic figure as far as he could remember. He particularly recalled one dream where she had been standing on a ledge halfway up a cliff with arms spread out sideways and draperies blowing in the wind. And he had been trying to climb to her—to rescue her perhaps—

only his fingers kept slipping on the rock and he never got any closer.

But that, he thought ruefully, didn't solve anything.

He stopped the car in the drive in front of the house instead of putting it away in the garage. Better get the windshield bit over straightaway. As he reached the front steps Kate came out of the door. She saw the splintered windshield immediately.

"Well, well," she sneered. "So much for your famous brilliance as a driver."

Stephen opened his mouth to defend himself but realized the pointlessness of it. Since childhood he and Kate had never had any time for each other. He clenched his jaw shut and pushed by her in silence.

Mr. Conway was in the lounge. Stephen went in.

"I'm afraid the windshield's gone," he said.

"However did that happen?" said Mr. Conway in his distressed voice, a thin high-pitched wail. His face puckered, almost as if he were going to cry. Stephen noticed that the sudden wrinkling of his face did not affect the smooth, shiny, bald skin on the top of his head.

"It just went," he said. "They do, you know. Something to do with the glass being stressed. There's a special clause in your insurance policy about replacing windshields."

"Are you sure?"

Stephen nodded. "Absolutely." He wasn't sure, but he knew the best way of dealing with his father. "I'll run right down and get it fixed if you like."

"I was thinking of using it later. . . ."

"There you are, then. Won't take long." Stephen got out of the house quickly and drove down to the garage.

While they were fitting the new glass he prowled for a while around the second-hand cars for sale, but he found his thoughts were wandering back to that strange incident on the hill. It was odd that the part he remembered most clearly was Bitta turning. He could still hear her voice speaking inside his head, a soft, feminine voice, and see the small delicate features, green eyes, long dark hair flowing in a luxurious cascade over her shoulders.

Suddenly he laughed aloud, for he recalled a ridiculous incident. He had been on holiday with the family, only last summer, at Dymchurch. One evening, he had gone for a long walk alone on the sand down near the edge of the quiet sea. He had been feeling lonely and in need of company but had been too shy to go into one of the crowded milk bars. And then, a long way away, he had seen this girl coming toward him, walking barefooted in the edge of the water.

First, he had seen the long dark hair. Then, as they approached each other, the almost-perfect features, the green eyes. He tried to think of something to say, something that would prevent them passing each other in silence. Something harmless and inoffensive so as not to frighten her. The time! He could ask the time. That was ordinary enough.

Then, as they came within a few feet of each other, he looked up again and saw with a shock that the young girl was in fact a woman of forty and that the long dark hair was a cardigan hanging limply across her shoulders.

"You can take it away now," said the garage mechanic.

"Eh?" Stephen jolted back to reality. "Oh, thanks."

"Remind your father to fill in his claims form. If we don't hear before the end of the month we'll be sending a bill."

"Yes," said Stephen. "Well, thanks again."

Four

As it happened, it was Mr. Wiggs's turn to take discussion group early on Monday afternoon. There were ten of them in the library, five arts people and five science. When initiating these periods and justifying their existence on an already crowded timetable, the headmaster had described them as "windows in the otherwise blank walls of the specialist's prison cell." Society, he said, had been busy producing scientists without a social conscience, irresponsible meddlers in the human condition, poets and artists whose understanding of the world compared unfavorably with that of Stone Age man. " 'Evil communications corrupt good manners,' " he quoted.

"A misapplied text if ever I heard one," Streeter had commented later. Streeter, of the slinky Mercedes, was a classics man. "But of course," he would say in answer to anyone's raised eyebrows, "anyone whose father runs a chain of shops selling potatoes and cabbages needs a good grounding in the classics."

"Belt up, Streeter," they said. They said it frequently; it was a sort of catch phrase.

This Monday, because Mr. Wiggs was leading the discussion, and also because Stephen had this muddled idea in his head, the talk inevitably drifted toward alternative worlds. Mr. Wiggs was eager to help. He felt that this was going to be one Monday that almost justified the headmaster's enthusiasm. He set about defining the space-time continuum.

"All right," said Stephen. "I suppose I understand in a sort of way."

"A neolithic sort of way," someone commented.

"Probably," Stephen admitted. "I gather that you're saying it's possible for two or more worlds to exist at the same time in the same space. . . ."

"That's oversimplifying," Wiggs interrupted. "It could only be true from the viewpoint of some infinitely remote observer. The two time scales might not be comparable. I suppose you could say some point in each scale might be said—from the observer's point of view —be said to coincide."

"'At the still point of the turning world,'" began Streeter.

"Belt up, Streeter," they said.

"Could an observer in one such world," said Stephen, "become aware of events in the other?"

"I don't really see how," Wiggs said. "Modern theory tends to see the observer as part of the action. And I can't see, even allowing for all the improbabilities we're taking in our stride, how you could get an interchange of energy between the two systems."

"Does seeing something involve energy?"

"Of course."

There was a short silence. Stephen said no more because he had reached the end of the line. Wiggs had said that what had happened up on the hill was impossible.

It was Mary who burst into the silence. It was as if she had been containing her pent-up feelings for too long. She poured the words over them—"like hot gravy," as Streeter said later.

"It's all so pointless," she cried. "I don't understand you all, sitting here and idly discussing the possibility of interfering in the affairs of some faintly possible other world. The whole of the earth's surface is a patchwork of other worlds. We know about them, but we behave as if they didn't exist. Black babies dying in South Africa for lack of protein, yellow babies dying in Vietnam from napalm burns, thousands of people in this country living like savages without food or shelter, war in this place, torture in that. Turn the TV on any night and one of these other worlds is there, just the other side of a sheet of glass. . . ."

She stopped, exhausted by her own indignation. The room had gone very quiet. No one looked at her. For the most part, they were staring blankly at their own hands or the tabletop.

Streeter said, "I don't see the relevance . . ." and then stopped, although no one had told him to.

After a while Wiggs cleared his throat. "I can see you feel this very deeply," he began. "Nevertheless . . ." He paused and blinked a couple of times. "No," he went on, "I think I'll leave you with the last word. It is almost time. . . ."

He looked at his watch, then gathered up his things and made for the door.

After a minute or two the others began to sort themselves out and get books for the next period. Only Mary, Streeter, and Stephen were left at the table.

"I've got a study period," said Stephen, going over to the shelves.

"So have I," said Streeter. "But I think I'll go down to town and get a haircut. There's a new shop just opened in Castle Street. If anybody asks for me, say I've gone to the museum."

Mary went on staring at nothing, scowling. Her sharp features had assumed a savage look. Stephen was suddenly reminded of the raw, torn whiteness of a damaged tree. He took a book from the shelf and opened it.

"You don't want to talk, do you?" she accused him.

"I don't want to fight," he said. "You've got all your hackles up."

He slid his finger down the index and stopped at "Crossbills." He turned to the page, found the paragraph, and read it. "Since 1910," he said. "You were right, then."

"About what?"

"About crossbills. It says here that since 1910 numbers of them have erupted from the continent every few years and nested in southeast England. They favor open coniferous woods but sometimes nest among scattered conifers on roadsides."

She stared at him for a moment as if he had given

utterance in an unknown tongue. Then she gave an abrupt laugh. "You're back on your hilltop," she accused him.

He shrugged his shoulders, grinning.

"Oh, all right. Get on with your essay and I'll get on with mine. Although what the world's sugar supply has to do with . . . oh, I suppose it has. Remotely."

She turned her attention away from him and opened her book.

Stephen turned the pages idly for a while, glancing at the colored pictures of birds, then he closed the book and went to return it to the shelf. The gap had been filled by the books on either side leaning together. He put his left hand in to spread them apart with his fingers. Beyond his hand, shining between his fingers, was a light. An electric light bulb, without a shade, hanging by a cord, against a gray background.

For a moment he could not bring his hand to act, then he was in control again. Instead of returning the bird book, he began to remove more books from the shelf with his left hand. At the back, where the brown paneling of the bookshelves should have been, was a window, and beyond the window a room.

Stephen's right hand, holding the heap of books, began to tremble. He looked at Mary, who was already concentrating on her work.

"Could you . . . could you spare a minute?" He had not intended his voice to sound so urgent.

Mary jumped up immediately and came over. "Are you all right?" she said. He recognized the concern in her voice and some instinct made him reject it.

"Of course I'm all right," he said brusquely. "I just can't find the *Oxford Dictionary*, that's all. And as you're always borrowing it for indefinite periods . . ."

Mary turned to the shelf. She picked out the dictionary and slammed it down hard on the pile of books he was holding. She went abruptly back to her table, pulling her books around so that she would be sitting with her back to him. She was furious with herself for letting him see how she felt.

Stephen put the books down quietly on the floor and turned his attention to the wall at the back of the shelf. Mary couldn't see the light but he could. Why? Because it's not there, was the obvious answer. He was hallucinating. And had been, back on the hill. Unless. Unless what? The threefold necessities again—place, time, and the individual. If the person who saw introduced some special element. Dreams were supposed to be wish-fulfilling. If he wanted to see . . . but how could he *want* to see an electric light bulb? He turned his attention more carefully to the hole in the bookcase.

It was a small room, almost empty, bare as a convent cell. The walls were flat-washed silver-gray, the color of a birch tree. There was no window, unless what he was looking through was one. There was a door on the right-hand wall. On the wall opposite were two shelves, a wide one to serve as a table or desk, and above it a short narrow shelf on which were arranged a number of flat green boxes, much the size and shape of tape-cassette boxes.

Stephen was disappointed. But then there was a swirl of movement and from right under him, under

39

his window, a girl stood up and reached over to the shelf for one of the boxes. She was in the center of the room, directly under the light, her head bent over the box.

She was so close Stephen felt embarrassed to be looking at her. He felt himself sway, as if he might be going to faint, and put a hand quickly on the shelf to steady himself. The girl did not look up. She was sliding up some sort of lid on the box and turning a dial. Then abruptly she pushed her hair back over her shoulder and threw herself down out of sight under the window.

"Bitta!" Stephen formed the word in his mind.

No answer came.

He could feel his heart thumping with excitement. He breathed deeply in an effort to steady himself, then leaned forward. First, he saw the edge of a mattress and an elbow and the green box, which he could now see was some sort of pad. Finally, when his forehead was pressing on the shelf above, he could see about half of her. She was lying on her right side with her right arm doubled under her head for a pillow. She was studying a panel in the box. It showed white lines of print. As she moved the dial the print slid up. Some sort of book, then.

He could look at her now. The shock and the embarrassment were wearing off. Her nostrils curved like the edge of a seashell, eyelids blue-veined with long brown lashes. Her hair was very dark and covered her shoulders. She moved her lips slightly as she read.

At one point she let the box lie flat on the bed. She picked her nose delicately with the little finger of her left hand, inspected her fingernail, and then wiped it on her hip. Stephen grinned to himself. He took the opportunity of trying to make out what was written on the pad and found to his surprise that it consisted of a series of oblong frames filled or partly filled with different numbers of dots. It was like no alphabet or language he had ever come across.

The girl rolled over and put both hands behind her head. She stared straight into Stephen's face. He wanted to smile or make some signal, some sort of communication, but his face remained stiff and expressionless as he stared back. He managed to raise one hand to make a sign of greeting, as if she were some way off, at least on the other side of the street. Her expression did not alter; her eyes were vacant. Obviously, it was not a two-way affair.

Mary Silver's voice broke in on him roughly. It had an edge of impatience as if she were speaking for the second time. "Are you sure you're all right?"

He dragged himself back from the shelves and turned to her.

"The look on your face," she said.

"What about it?"

He was angry with her for catching him. He scowled, waiting for her ridicule. Hurriedly he replaced the books on the shelf and lined them up.

"Nothing," she said, quick to recognize her own trespass. "I thought you were supposed to be doing an essay." She felt the cold wind of loneliness across her shoulders. Serves you right, she told herself—it's obvious he doesn't want anything to do with you. Why do you keep trying?

Stephen drifted in an aimless fashion about the room,

coming to rest at the window, which overlooked the front drive. Wiggs had said any exchange between the two worlds was impossible. But there had been some sort of exchange in the car. Which could just mean Wiggs was wrong. Or it could mean the girl did not inhabit some unreachable space-time other-world. She had not seen him. Green eyes. He felt a tremor of warmth and shot his head around to make sure Mary was not staring at him. She was bent over the table, one sharp shoulder blade pushing up under her cardigan like a ridge of rock close under the turf. If he could get into that cell, perhaps—he went out of the library and closed the door quietly behind him.

On the left, where the cell door would be, was a door marked STAFF TOILET. Seldom used. The library was isolated from the busier parts of the school. He listened at the door for a moment, keeping an eye on the staircase. Then he went in.

Oddly enough, it was almost the same size as the cell. He looked immediately to where the bed would have been, but of course there was nothing; nothing he could see, or presumably touch. But something was in there; other senses assured him of it.

"Who is it? It's you, Curwen!" The voice in his head was sharp, suspicious. He had breached her privacy and she resented it. "What are you doing here?"

He wasn't sure how to speak to her. Would thinking do? He spoke aloud, for lack of knowledge.

"My name is Stephen," he said simply.

"Stephen? Do I know you?"

"No. Not really."

"Then go away, please."

Stephen turned obediently to the door, but then, sensing some doubt in her mind, paused there and waited.

"Stephen?"

"I'm still here."

"Yes, I know. Is this some sort of a trick? Or a test perhaps?"

"Not that I know of."

"How did you come?"

"Through the door." He grinned to himself. "The usual way."

"You can see me?"

"Not now. I could a little while ago. I think you're very good-looking . . . well . . . beautiful, really." The things one dared to say, safely invisible. Better than a telephone.

He felt a sudden jumbling of his thoughts, a blurring, painful in a queer way, and then nothing.

"She's hung up!" he said aloud, because that was just what it felt like. I must be going around the bend, he thought, chatting away to myself.

The room felt chilly, hostile, as if trying to get rid of him.

"Bitta!" he said. "Are you still there?"

There was no answer.

He seemed to be standing in the center of nowhere—a great, empty, deserted world. All around stood the clutter of dead objects, walls, doors, furniture, buildings, even people, all empty and dried. Husks.

In the disfigured street
He left me, with a kind of valediction,
And faded on the blowing of the horn.

43

The words drifted through his mind but he could not remember where they had come from. He could not be sure that he had ever known. He felt, for a desolating moment, like the only living thing on the vast surface of some dead planet.

Instead of going back to the library he went out onto the playing field. Most of the area was taken up with second-year classes noisily enjoying a games period, but there was a place beyond the swimming pool, behind a row of newly planted birch trees, where one could relax without interruption. He made his way there, telling himself that he was not really slacking; he simply had to get his thoughts straight.

But stretched out on the warm grass, he made no effort to think. His taut muscles relaxed in the sun. His mind began to drift without definite direction. For a moment he had a picture of Mary's shoulder blade projecting sharply under her cardigan.

Mary Silver! Streeter had taken her out one evening. What was it he'd said the next day? "You have to like wearing a hair shirt to spend an evening with her. She's the most abrasive person I know. I thought she was going to sharpen my wits but she just ground them down to the quick!"

Stephen smiled to himself. All the same, when he thought of Mary he had a vague feeling of guilt. He let his thoughts slide away into warmer country.

Dark hair and the long stretch of the beach. This time it really would be her. Bitta was a strange name. Saxon? Not with all that dark hair. He let the distant figure come closer.

A shadow fell across him and he opened his eyes and sat up quickly. "It would be you!" he exclaimed irritably.

"What do you mean, it would be me?" Mary was taken aback.

"Oh, sorry," he mumbled. "I was half asleep. What's up?"

"Lunchtime," she said. "I happened to see you going across the field." She turned her back abruptly and walked quickly away.

Five

Three of them walked up from the bus as usual—Stephen, Margaret, and Margaret's friend Sally. The two girls were having a good time laughing together about some private joke. Stephen realized that most of their enjoyment came from his not knowing what the joke was. The girls kept exchanging mysterious and oblique bits of conversation and laughing uncontrollably. Stephen walked a couple of paces ahead of them, brushing one hand along the hedge as he went, enjoying the sharp sting of the leaves against his skin.

Halfway up the hill a couple of men were forking bitumen into a number of small breaks in the road's surface. The bitumen, heated in a small, rather primitive boiler, was giving out dense white fumes. Stephen lingered a minute or so to breathe near the boiler. The girls ran quickly past.

"Choke yourself on that stuff," one of the men warned, turning his black and gleaming fork over and leaning on the handle.

"I like it," Stephen said.

"Kills germs off, I'll say that for it," the man agreed. "Never get a cold."

Stephen grinned and walked on. The girls had stopped at the corner of the lane where Sally turned off. As he came up to them they separated.

"Ask him," Sally called back. "Go on, I dare you!"

Margaret laughed but did not answer. She turned to wait for Stephen and they walked on, side by side, for some distance without speaking.

Margaret obviously had something to say and was having trouble finding the right opening. It would have been easier if Stephen had shown curiosity. At last she began, "Sally thinks . . ."

"You amaze me," said Stephen.

"Oh, very witty. She thinks Mary Silver likes you."

"Then she's probably quite right. I like Mary Silver."

"You know I didn't mean that. I meant specially. She's all hung up about you. At least, Sally says so."

"I wonder where she gets her information from."

"She said she's noticed her looking at you when you didn't know she was, and she had a sort of yearning look on her face."

Stephen plodded on in silence.

"Is something going on between you two, I mean?"

Stephen snorted. "If there was," he said, "we'd be pretty careful to keep it from your fat little friend."

"Sally's not fat. Well, not unusually. She's well developed."

"Is that what it's called?" Stephen laughed.

"Well, at least it's more normal than being like Mary Silver," Margaret said crossly. She was more self-conscious about Sally's shape than Sally was herself.

"Mary's all right," Stephen said. "What does it matter anyway what shape people are? I mean, Mary's about as graceful as a tent peg but she's easy to get on with. She doesn't obtrude."

Margaret let out a shout of laughter.

"I meant her personality. She's not pushy."

He was furious with himself though, for allowing himself to be drawn into such a discussion. You could never unsay a thing. And it was worse when you found you'd been provoked into saying something you didn't believe. Mary Silver was not easy to get on with. Far from it.

They walked the rest of the way in silence.

All that evening Stephen was restless. He could settle down to nothing. It was such an undefined uneasiness; very different from a specific worry.

"Are you sickening for something?" his mother asked at one point.

"He's in love," said Margaret.

"I don't know what it is," he said. "I think I'll see if I can walk it off."

"Take the dog," said his father. "I don't think he's had any exercise at all today."

Stephen did not answer this. He had no intention of taking the dog, which was a wirehaired terrier, almost uncontrollable. It pounced on smaller dogs and shook them silly, picked fights with bigger dogs, and had to be rescued, smeared with blood, and apologized for. It also had an unpleasant smell. Stephen hated it with a fixed hatred.

48

It followed him to the door and nipped his ankle as he tried to slide out. From the garden he heard it setting up a hysterical noise, so he ran for it—down the garden, over the wall behind the garage, and into the nettles and overgrown grass beyond.

That way lay the gravel pits, disused, overgrown, strewn with the rusting remains of gas stoves, bicycles, prams, and bedsteads. The largest pit had become a lake with its own pair of nesting swans.

Stephen walked around this area for half an hour. He saw a couple lying on a raincoat; they heard him coming and stared at him until he had gone self-consciously past. At this point he caught a glimpse of the river, a misted mirror in the moonlight, and turned toward it. He crossed the road by the convent. A long, tongue-shaped field reaching out to the water was reputed to be a Roman causeway, built in the days when the river was deep and tidal, and oceangoing galleys docked there and unloaded goods for Canterbury.

Stephen stood in the long, damp grass, looking down toward the water and trying to imagine the comings and goings of those days without any great success. He did not have that sort of imagination. History for him was a set of statements in books. And yet, although his mind resisted picturing the past, he did feel uncomfortably aware of people close around him, crowding him, but not in a threatening way. In the middle of an open field he had a feeling of claustrophobia.

He looked about him, but apart from the lights of a single car away over on the hills there was no sign of a human being anywhere. He walked slowly down the field, the old causeway, and the feeling eased a little, as if he had walked out of a room full of silent people into a little open space. There was a stile at the end of the field. He climbed it and then sat on the step and leaned his back on the bar.

Below was the river, flooded at this point where gravel was washed and dredged by a gaunt machine standing clear of the water now, like some monster left over from the age of giant reptiles. Beyond, the land climbed, and on the top of the ridge stood the small group of pine trees. He must be sitting, he now realized, just about where the buildings had been in that strange picture seen through the windshield from the top of the hill. Under those very pines in fact. Where Mary Silver said she had fallen and broken her leg. And now he was in the middle of it.

For a moment the landscape slid before his eyes, as if moving in the moonlight. His mind seemed to slide with it; a pleasurable giddiness, like the sensation just before fainting, as if contact with the visible world was being lost. He closed his eyes and leaned his head back against the wood of the stile, which was no longer hard wood but something soft that allowed his head to sink back in a more comfortable position.

I mustn't go to sleep here, he thought to himself and at the same time he was letting go, falling, falling. . . .

Six

He slept uneasily until dawn and then, as the first hard ray of light cut like a knife blade between the shutters, he fell at last into a deep and restful sleep. When he woke again the shutters had been thrown back and the room was filled with sunlight. He was alone in the room; the other three beds not only were empty but had been made up.

He sat up cautiously, expecting to feel dizzy, but in fact, he discovered very quickly, he was filled with a pleasant feeling of general well-being. He even hummed to himself as he went down the long tiled corridor to the shower room. The faintest smell of coffee, drifting across the courtyard from the kitchens, started his mouth watering. He showered and dressed quickly. His bed was in a sad disorder after his night of restless dreaming and he had to strip it right down to make it properly.

Even so, he was striding across the courtyard a few minutes later, looking with approval at the very solid blue of the sky, smiling at the brilliantly flowering azaleas in their elaborately molded earthenware pots.

All but one of the long refectory tables had been cleared and scrubbed. He apologized at the counter when he went for his breakfast but the girl gave him a friendly smile as she served him.

"Glad to see you back," she said.

He took his tray and sat down opposite one of the two men still eating.

"You're back, then," the man said. He was a heavy-shouldered man of about thirty named Wint. He was well known in the commune for his rather sardonic view of life. "I was laying odds you'd stay."

"And do what?"

"Well, anything. There are jobs in the city for them that care for that sort of life."

"I wouldn't leave the commune," Stephen said.

"People do."

"Not me. I love it here. Where could you live better than the way we do?"

Wint laughed. "All right. You don't have to sell it to me. I just thought . . . well, I mean, you took Bitta in, didn't you? And you didn't exactly hurry back. It simply occurred to me you might have decided to work there so as to be near her."

"But she's gone into the Sike College," exclaimed Stephen. "It's five years' training, so what would be the point? Oh, and anyway . . ."

"All the same, I'm surprised," Wint said. "I thought you two were inseparable."

Stephen looked at his breakfast tray and found he

was no longer as hungry as he'd thought. "She didn't have to go," he said.

"People who are lucky enough to have that sort of gift always do go," Wint said. "At least, in my experience. Which is just as well. Where would we be without the sikes?" He picked up his tray to carry it across to the counter. "So love's young dream is sadly shattered, is it?" he added with a return of his usual cynical manner.

"You could put it that way," Stephen said with a half-grin. "Although to tell you the truth Bitta seemed so changed, once she had this idea in her head, that she might have been another person. In fact you could say the relationship was between two other people—not us at all."

"So it's all over and forgotten, then?"

"I shall have to see her once more, I think. Have to make a clean break. Otherwise our minds will be cluttered up with the past."

"Just as well, if you want my opinion," Wint said. "These sikes, they're not really normal people, once they've really begun to concentrate. They're like . . . in another dimension, if you see what I mean. They don't live our life or think our thoughts. They're like creatures from another world. They only make contact when they're straightening out some bent mind."

They took their trays to the counter and went out together into the sun-warmed air. Already the heady smell of eucalyptus and mimosa drifted down the valley. The pleasant geometry of the fish ponds promised the coolness of blue water. Beyond rose the sharp slope of tangled scrub and outcrops of yellow rock, beginning already to writhe in the heat haze, and at the top of the slope, etched clear against the dark blue of the sky, stood the four huge carob trees—so clear that even the hanging pods of last year's fruit could be seen like rows of commas beneath each branch.

Wint nodded and started down the track toward the pumping station. Stephen waited a moment, breathing deep lungfuls of the untainted air. His usual feeling of joy in each morning's beginning came back to him. Blue-clad figures moved busily about the ponds, carrying out their tasks for the day, and he only delayed joining them because he wanted to savor the pleasures of anticipation.

From behind, a little way up the slope, came the sound of children's voices and a woman saying, "It's an easy word. Make the sounds. What's this letter? Four little dots, one in each corner. What sound does that make?"

Stephen smiled to himself and went down toward the hatcheries where he was working on experimental hybrids. The other five men already working there smiled and nodded to him, pleased to see him back.

Orin called over, "You're in a hurry to get back to work, aren't you?"

The man working with Orin gave his elbow a nudge and muttered something Stephen did not catch. Orin's cheerful smile changed to an expression of sympathy, the way you might look at someone whose best friend had died. Then he raised his shoulders and spread his hands; a gesture which plainly meant, "What you can't change you must learn to accept."

For the next hour Stephen concentrated all his attention on the job. He netted the great golden fish one by one, gently squeezed out the eggs into the shallow fertilizing trays, and placed each tray on the moving belt which carried them to the next pond. This particular hybrid experiment was aiming at combining the size of one fish and the delicate flavor of the other. As the two fish came from different oceans with different salinity and different temperatures, the problem was a tricky one. So far, the fertility rate of the eggs was consistently lower than twelve percent.

Whenever he paused to rest and stretch his back he found his eyes drawn to the group of carobs on the ridge. He had an odd, uneasy feeling that in some way they were threatening him. It niggled at his enjoyment of the day and the work, and at his general feeling of well-being. As the morning wore on he grew uneasier.

"Orin," he said at one point, "look up at those trees, will you?"

His friend came over. "The carobs?"

Stephen nodded but kept his own eyes down on what he was doing.

"What about them?"

"Do you feel anything? As if we were being . . . well . . . watched?"

"No."

"Do you feel anything odd?"

Orin laughed. "Only in the way you're acting. What's the matter, then?"

"I don't know. Imagination, I guess."

"You haven't caught something, have you? Do you

remember Samly? They said it was from not washing up properly after handling some of those big old fish. He acted in a very queer way for a few days." Orin was concerned.

"No. It's not that sort of feeling. Forget it. I expect I'm a bit edgy."

Orin privately thought it was something to do with his separation from Bitta and his two days in the city. "What about a game of chess at lunchtime?" he said. "I've got a move that'll fix that King's Indian of yours."

"Good idea," Stephen said. Each went back to his work.

The men strolled back to the canteen for the mid-morning break. One or two sat outside to sip their cool drinks in the sun, but most of them went inside and sat around the tables. Although they worked as a team each one worked alone, so that break time was a period for social living, conversation, making music, games. There were no special limits put on these periods. In the commune, people worked because they enjoyed it and wanted to.

This morning, Stephen and Orin took their drinks outside. But they had been sitting less than five minutes when Stephen felt that the threat from the distant group of trees was too strong to remain unanswered any longer.

"I'm going up there," he told Orin. "If I'm not back in half an hour check the temperature in M tank for me, will you?"

"Would you like me to come with you?"

"I'd rather go alone—thanks for offering though."

"I'll check the tank, then. No need to rush."

Beyond the ponds the land was untended and wild. The ridge was mostly of a sandy gravel between the rocky places, and little grew except creeping succulents, stunted she-oaks, and the inevitable patches of cactus. A number of narrow footpaths or goat tracks zigzagged up the slope but not with any definite purpose. Stephen made his way with considerable care. Some of the cactus leaves were tipped with hard black thorns longer than fingers, capable of piercing to the bone.

Tiny honey-eaters whirred away as he approached the top of the hill. Enamel-bright lizards gaped at the intruder for a fraction of a second before shooting in one scarlet flash for the nearest cover. The sun, now nearing its midday heat, beat down on him; his blue work tunic was darkened with patches of sweat.

The four carobs stood in a close group, roots and branches entwined. The ground under them was crusty with seed pods. The heavy foliage gave a shade so cool it was like plunging into cold water. Stephen stopped for a moment or so, leaning on one of the trunks, easing the sticky cloth away from his shoulder blades. Cicadas that had stopped their racket as he approached started up again as soon as he was still.

Uneasiness seemed to be in the very air, akin to the feeling just before a storm. This was not general but directed only at him. He had somehow expected to see Bitta up here—against all reason, since he had left her in the city the previous day. Perhaps he felt this because it was here they had stood when Bitta told him the news that she had been chosen for training in the college.

He looked about him suspiciously. No, not quite here. About twenty paces away was a small stone hut with a black doorless opening. It was a storeroom, in fact, containing fire-fighting appliances and a small hand siren. That was where they had stood, he now remembered, just inside, in the cool shade of the doorway. He moved toward it and as he did so the threat seemed to gather strength.

As he neared the entrance his heart began to beat faster. There were no windows in the hut and the interior should have been in deep shadow. In fact it glowed with dim, pearly-gray light. He put one hand on the hot stone and slowly leaned forward. What he saw made him jerk back in surprise. He went to the front of the hut; the stone face was unbroken. No aperture or window interrupted the sheer surface. He went back to the entrance and this time walked more boldly inside.

Light seemed to be coming through an opening, where he knew there was none. At least at first he thought it was only light, then he saw that it was a heavily clouded sky, such as he had never in his life seen before. He moved forward and saw land, a river valley, but not the valley as he knew it. This valley had no bright clear light and hard colors. It was a scene of utter desolation. The river was flooded, and ungainly machines, ugly with rust, groped and scoured beneath the water. On the far side of the water, where the modest commune buildings ought to have been, the land was scratched and tortured out of all recognition. Huge areas of woodland and orchard had disappeared and in their place hundreds of ugly, brittle houses were jammed so close to each other that each patch looked like a discolored scab on the back of the living hillside. Running roughly parallel with the line of the river, and still on the far side, was some sort of road, sealed over with a hard surface which gave off, in the water-laden air, a sulky, steely shine. And on this road—far wider than any he had ever seen—ran a constant stream of metal vehicles which emitted a thin, evil-looking vapor and seemed to be taking part in a frantic race, winking red and orange lights, swinging out of line in order to pass one another, hurrying constantly with the stupid urgency of ants.

Feeling sickened at this strange vision, Stephen began to back away. At that moment a girl appeared, as if she had walked past the side of the hut within a few inches of him. She turned for a moment and her mouth moved, although no sound reached him. She was strangely dressed, rather thin, with short fair hair, and a sharp, eager face—not by any standards particularly pretty and yet a face that held Stephen's attention because of something attractive that lay behind it.

He just had time to notice that she was bleeding from a small cut above her wrist and that her garments were speckled with drops of blood, when she turned and ran rapidly out of sight down the hill. He walked quickly out of the hut as if he thought he might catch another glimpse of her, but the scene was the one he was familiar with, and there was no one on the path leading downhill.

He did not look inside the hut again, but walked slowly and thoughtfully back toward the commune.

Seven

After lunch Stephen went to see the director of the farm.

"Good to see you back, Curwen," said the director. "I was getting worried you might have been accepted too."

The director was against the yearly sievings; he lost good workers and the farm worked on a minimum of staff. He was also against the purpose of the sievings. The sikes were all very well in their way and no doubt did a great deal of good, but out here, in the easygoing outdoor life of the farm, they hadn't had more than one case of a hang-up in ten years, and that one drowned himself before the sikes could be brought out.

"I want to go in to the center," Stephen said. "Can I take the transport?"

"But you've only just come from there. Why do you want to go back? Isn't that asking for trouble?"

"I want to see Bitta again!"

The director looked worried. "Wouldn't it be

better to wait a few more days?"

The director's face showed his unhappiness. He knew about the close relationship these two youngsters shared. "These blasted sievings," he muttered. "They go on about the value to the community of the Sike Colleges —selection procedure a hundred percent efficient—and so on and so on. They never weigh it up against the damage that's done."

"I suppose I could walk," Stephen said.

The director laughed. "Oh, all right, then. Take the transport. But for goodness' sake . . ."

"I know. Drive carefully and don't damage the paint-work."

"You know I wasn't thinking about the machine."

Stephen grinned and left the office.

He sprinted across to the hangar with a feeling of elation. At least he was doing something instead of standing about worrying. The transport was already on the ramp, the mechanic climbing down and wiping off his fingers on a grubby piece of cotton waste.

"You taking her out?"

"Yes, I've seen the director."

"But you won't mind if I check?"

"Of course not."

As the mechanic walked over to the intercom Stephen climbed up into the transport. The helmet was dangling by its straps on the controls. He put it on and adjusted the spacers for comfort. When he had the seat straps clicked around him he looked down. The mechanic was coming away from the intercom. He grinned and held a thumb up. Stephen waved.

61

He pressed down the switch to bring in the center beacon, operated the autocontrol and then the fire button. The machine took off in a beautiful, exhilarating, upward curve, leveled off at the statutory height, swung a little until it was central on the beacon, and then settled down.

In less than five minutes he was approaching the center port. When the panel light flashed he flicked up the autocontrol switch. The transport wriggled slightly, like a dog wagging its tail; the port landers had taken over. A moment later he heard the retros fire and felt the transport dropping down toward the pad in a delightful, slow-motion fall, as if going down through water. The touch was just perceptible.

He identified himself at the Inward desk. A bored clerk added the details to a long list in front of him.

"Purpose?"

Stephen hesitated. "Well, I want to make some inquiries about someone who was accepted at the last sieving."

"You and a couple of hundred others," murmured the clerk, making a code mark in the "purpose" column of his list. "Try Information. Straight down the center tunnel. You can't miss it."

On the far side of the vestibule were ranged five circular openings, the entrances to tunnels leading to different sectors of the center. He took the middle one and found himself after a few minutes in a large circular patio busy with people. Around the circumference were cafés, restaurants, shops. In the center a large transparent hemisphere was labeled INFORMATION. He went in through the nearest arch and approached the first vacant desk. Behind it sat a plump girl with an eager, questing look. Her contact lenses bulged so much that when she blinked, her eyelids were slowed midway in their descent, thus adding an odd sultriness to her eager efficiency.

When Stephen had told the girl what he wanted she looked disappointed.

"I'm afraid we're never given any information about the new entrants," she said. "At least, not until the course has started. We have lists of new sikes in training, but your friend wouldn't have got that far yet, would she?"

"I suppose not."

"If I were you I'd start at the beginning and just work through the departments until one of them comes up with something."

Stephen looked appalled. "That might take days!"

The girl laughed. "I didn't mean *write*," she said. "I mean, you only want to *know*, don't you? You don't want a permanent *record*?"

"I just want to know. And I'd like to see her if possible."

"It shouldn't take more than a few minutes to find out where she is," said the girl. "Use this." She picked up a hoop of wire from the desk and held it out to him.

"How?"

"Start at the reception block. They'll tell you where she went. Then just follow up."

Stephen lifted the hoop of wire and inspected it. It was just a simple hoop about a hand's width across with two small colored pads attached. A thin thread connected it to a box on the desk.

"What is it?" he said at last.

"A thoughtfone, of course." The girl looked at him as if he'd suddenly grown horns or a third eye or something.

"I've never used one."

The girl's eye bulged even more. "You're joking?"

"I live on a commune, you see. A bit too basic for this sort of thing." He felt a proper country bumpkin saying this, and yet not without an odd twinge of pride.

"On a commune!" the girl exclaimed. "Oh, aren't you *lucky*! I applied two or three years ago, but of course I didn't stand a *chance*. You have to be so *frantically* fit to be taken."

"Hard luck. Still, you might not have liked it."

"Oh, I'm sure I would have." The girl sat with a remote and blissful look on her face for a few seconds and then snapped back suddenly into her role as information clerk. "Well, they're absolutely *simple* to use. I'll show you."

She took the hoop out of his hand and put it over his head, adjusting the two pads to press on his brow just above his eyes. "The red one goes over the right eye," she said. "That's *all* you have to remember. Now you just *think* of the Reception Block—no, you can't do that because I don't suppose you know what it *looks* like—just think of the number seventeen because that's their number. Make a *picture* of it in your head. You can close your eyes if you like. Some people find it easier. And when the operator comes up you just *think* what you want to say. Once you've done it you'll see how easy it is."

"Why can't I just think of my friend?" Stephen asked. "It would save a lot of time."

The girl laughed. "It's not *magic*," she said. "It's only a machine."

Stephen closed his eyes. He had only just started to get a mental picture of the number seventeen when it was at once replaced by a picture of a dark-haired woman sitting in front of a bank of switches.

"Yes," she said.

Stephen tried to formulate in his mind what he would have said had he been standing at the desk.

"Your thoughts are not organized," the woman said, but not critically; more as if it were something she often had to say.

Stephen tried again and this time the woman seemed to understand. She consulted some lists that were pinned to the wall on her right.

"Kept here for eight hours," she said, her finger holding the place, "transferred to Test Center. Try there—227."

Stephen opened his eyes. The girl behind the desk was watching him with interest. "All right?" she said.

"It's marvelous," Stephen said, impressed by the apparatus.

The girl grunted. "Some people just can't organize their thoughts," she said. "You don't know *what* they want. The inside of their heads, just like a junk shop. But otherwise it's quite a handy thing."

Stephen nodded. "Well, excuse me," he said politely

and closed his eyes again. It was rather like submerging, he thought. You really ought to hold your nose as well. He pictured 227.

A different girl at another bank of switches came up. "Yes?"

This time he stated his thoughts quickly and without confusion. The girl also consulted her lists.

"The young lady is resting at the moment. You could fone her at three-thirty."

"I'd rather come and see her. It that allowed?"

"Of course. If you go to the cloisters and wait there I'll pass a message to her."

"The cloisters?"

"Of course." She blacked out and Stephen opened his eyes again. He removed the hoop and handed it back.

"Success?" asked the girl.

"I'm to meet her in the cloisters," he said, frowning.

"She's still being tested, then."

"Yes, but—what did she mean, 'cloisters'?"

"The cathedral, of course. Where else would she be? It's the cathedral staff that run the tests. The dean is also the principal of the Sike College."

Stephen thanked the girl for helping him. He was just leaving when she said, "I shouldn't worry about it. I mean, those sikes do an absolutely *wonderful* job. They save thousands of people every year. If your friend is selected for training she'll be very lucky."

"Have you ever had to go to a sike?"

"Well, no. But a friend of mine got very warped a year or so ago and she went. She was an *awful* mess. Suicidal and everything. But they straightened her out."

"Thanks," said Stephen.

He found he had time to spare before going to the cathedral so he sat down at one of the bright little tables in the patio and ordered a fruit juice and a plate of sweet biscuits. They weren't as good as the commune cook's efforts in that line but he sat, sipping and munching, watching the busy scene in front of him, and managing to feel relaxed. After all, it wasn't any good worrying. He would just have to wait and see.

Eight

The cloisters were rich with sun and shadow. The peace and stability the old builders had aimed at still hung over the worn mellow stone. The soaring arches of the cathedral itself and the rich carving of the south porch were both excluded from the cloisters. Here the scale was human, reassuring. The eye rested on the quiet, undemanding stone surfaces; the mind relaxed and was at home.

Stephen came early and walked slowly up and down on the north side. The sun came through each arch with an explosive warmth. Looking through, across grass and water, to the shadowed southern cloister he could see a few people moving, pacing slowly, heads down, weaving in and out like fish in a shady pool.

A sequence of bells sounded from a distance and he saw by his watch that it was half past three. Any of the dimly seen figures on the far side could have been Bitta, but rather than walk around to find out he sat down in the full sun with his back against the warm stone of a pillar, half closed his eyes, and waited.

A few moments later he had the uneasy feeling of being watched. He had been facing the central green. Now he turned his head sharply to find Bitta seated across the arch from him and regarding him with a steady, unblinking gaze. He moved to get up but she half raised one hand in a gesture that seemed to tell him to stay where he was. He sank back and inspected her for a few seconds without speaking.

She was dressed entirely in white, a soft enveloping gown that left visible only her face and her hands—which lay forgotten in her lap, palm uppermost, slightly curled, like two leaves that had drifted there from an autumn tree, and her feet in white cord sandals. Her heavy dark hair was braided and hung forward over her left shoulder. Her green eyes regarded him with a steady, neutral gaze.

At first Stephen was disappointed. He did not know how he had expected her to react to his coming so soon, but certainly not with this nothing-look. All this must have shown in his face, for she gave the faintest shadow of a smile. There was a quality in that smile that had never belonged in their relationship before; sympathy, was it? or compassion? It made him feel that his journey here had been quite pointless. He had nothing whatever to say to her.

All the same he heard himself speaking. "Wint says that you people are like visitors from another world."

"You are the visitor," she said, and her voice seemed to come from infinitely far away. "You may come a few more times—as long as the ways are open. But in the end you must decide."

"I don't really understand what you're talking about,

but as to deciding—I think I've done that."

"No," she said. "Not yet. Go back now, and later on you will know for certain what you want to do. There will be a time for choosing."

Her voice was spreading out, like smoke blowing through trees in the orchard. The words seemed bodiless, parched, the mere sketchy outlines of sound. And then he thought she said, "Good-bye, Stephen."

His mind drifted around the word in an idly curious way. "Stephen?" he said inwardly. "Who the devil is Stephen?"

But he was drifting downward in slow circles like an autumn leaf on a day of no wind. He tried to reach out, as if his thought were a hand to clutch at a passing branch.

"My name is . . ." But the thought failed to pluck a conclusion and the circling leaf reached the ground.

Nine

Every Wednesday evening one or the other of the Silver family went over to see their grandmother. When Mary volunteered to go out of turn her mother was surprised.

"It's not your turn for another fortnight," she said.

" 'Let it go which way it will, he that dies this year is quit for the next.' "

"Who's talking about dying?"

"Shakespeare was."

"Oh, him! I might have known. Anyway, I'll tell you something; your gran's a long way from dying. All the women in our family have lived into their nineties. So you can save up your bits of Shakespeare for another ten years at least."

"Let's skip it, Mum, shall we? I didn't mean it that way."

"Wouldn't do any harm if you said what you did mean, now and then."

Mary sighed. She never got on very well with her

mother. She always felt it was her own fault but didn't know what to do about it. "Well, I did start off by saying I'd be the one to go over tonight. That's plain enough surely?"

"It may sound plain enough," said her mother sharply. "What I'm wondering is why? You never do go over more often than you can help."

"As a matter of fact," said Mary, and then grinned suddenly to herself, remembering Stephen saying that anyone who started a statement with "As a matter of fact" or "To be absolutely frank" or any other equivalent phrase was usually about to disburden himself of a truly fruity lie. As she was, at this moment.

"As a matter of fact what?"

"As a matter of fact," she repeated with relish, "I've got to do an essay on living standards before the first World War. I thought Gran would be able to help."

"She'll do that, all right. Keep you there till midnight, rambling on. But you want to take it with a pinch of salt. She gets her years muddled up something dreadful."

Mrs. Silver was busying herself with packing various parcels into the large shopping basket. "Well then," she said. "If you're set on going you'd better go. The bus is due in ten minutes. Don't bang the basket about because there's eggs in it."

"Have I got to take that great load?" Mary exclaimed in disgust. "Proper Little Red Riding Hood act, this is. Anyway it's ridiculous. Gran gets fresher eggs than we do. And she likes making cakes. Where's the sense in sending her a cake? If you want to help her why not just send her some money?"

"You know very well she wouldn't take it. And anyway, when you're an old lady of eighty-two you'll be pleased to have little attentions paid you. The trouble with children nowadays is they never think of anyone but themselves. When I was your age we didn't have . . ."

"If I'm going to catch that bus I'd better run," said Mary grabbing the basket and getting out of the kitchen as fast as she could.

"Why do I keep arguing?" she asked herself as she hurried to the bus stop. "I need to have my head examined. Why don't I just say 'Yes, Mum' and 'No, Mum'? It'd save a lot of time and energy."

When the bus came it was nearly empty. Mary had hoped to be able to sit quietly, straightening out her own rather muddled thoughts, but the bus conductor was bored and in a chatty mood, so by the time she got off at the turning she was no nearer understanding her own motives in suddenly coming out to see her grandmother.

The lane leading up the slope past her grandmother's house went back across the river over the old stone bridge. The afternoon had been dull with a steady drizzle, but now, an hour or so before sunset, the clouds were being briskly swept out to sea. In front of her, where the lane climbed twisting up the slope, there was already a thin blue showing beyond the ridge, outlining the group of old pines with a sort of halo. The air smelled of fresh green, of river water, and of wood smoke. Mary sniffed at it appreciatively.

The cottage stood on the bank. Mary climbed the steps and pushed her way through the laurustinus bushes on the left of the pretentious little curly-iron gate. Even now she could remember that argument there'd been when her mother had been obsessed with the idea of getting a wrought-iron gate.

"Are we going to have a butler as well?"

"I don't know what you mean."

"Well, wrought iron! It just doesn't belong, that's what I mean. We don't live at Woburn Abbey or Penshurst Place, that's what I mean. Why do we have to pretend?"

"I'm not pretending. I just want a wrought-iron gate. I think they're nice. Lots of people have them. Honestly, you do get some queer ideas."

"Well, I'm not going to use it," Mary said, carried past common sense by her failure to communicate.

And she never had. She'd made herself a pathway through the bushes, a pathway the postman and the milkman soon took to using.

"Now look what you've done," her mother had objected. "You and your silly ideas."

"It just shows their instincts are right."

"Oh no it doesn't," her father had said, making one of his rare contributions to the discussion. "It's because they've got their hands full and it's easier."

Mary stood now inside the garden and, smiling gently to herself, looked around at the familiar scene. It was odd that she liked to come back here; something she could never truly understand. It wasn't as if she had been particularly happy. The cottage was small and they'd been vilely overcrowded. There had always been friction, especially with her mother. But that hadn't changed. And when she'd passed the examinations . . .

"But you won't want to go to that private school, will you?"

"Of course I do."

"You won't be happy there. They're not our sort."

"That's stupid. They're not any special sort. They're just cleverer, that's all."

"Suppose we say we can't afford it? Where would you be then? Miss High-and-Mighty, aren't you? Cleverer, she says! Well, if cleverness goes with rudeness . . ."

Then her father's voice, wearily from behind his newspaper: "Of course she can go if she wants to. We'll manage somehow."

"His master's voice, is it? She can go, just like that! What do you mean, we can manage? Who's the one who'll have to do the managing, that's what I want to know. It's all very well for you to sit there and . . ."

The usual dreary squabble. Mary had slipped away, feeling guilty but defiant. She'd show them!

The trouble was she hadn't been able to. Hadn't been able to justify her father's support, for he had died while she was still halfway through her first year. And when she tried to remember him with gratitude she found there was so little of him left to remember. He was always such a quiet, unemphatic man, living most of the time in some world of his own.

And all those years since, with just her mother. What a silly business it all was—families, relations. Pity the pack couldn't be reshuffled now and then so that the groups ended up in different combinations. There couldn't be two more ill-matched people, she and her mother. Not if you shuffled the pack for a hundred years.

"The ugly-duckling syndrome," she thought grimly as she turned to face her grandmother's cottage. "Or perhaps the ugly-duckling-is-really-a-swan syndrome, if there is such a thing. Suppose they're right and I'm not a swan? What happens to the ugly ducklings that grow up to be ugly ducks? You never hear about them, but there must be millions of them. I'd rather like to hear what Stephen would have to say about that."

She walked around the side of the house—the front door being invariably bolted, chained, and blocked up with brooms and buckets—tapping on the kitchen window as she passed. She saw her grandmother, seated at the scrubbed kitchen table, look up expectantly and smile.

Inside the back porch Mary suddenly realized why she had come. She was amused at the wily dishonesty that had prevented her until now of being fully aware of her own motives.

"Hullo, Gran," she said cheerfully as she opened the door. "Enter Little Red Riding Hood."

"If you've got more of those nasty stale supermarket eggs in the basket," said the old lady, "you can take them back. I made cakes of the last lot and you could still taste them."

"I told Mum you could get better ones."

"Well, of course I can. Whatever was she thinking of?"

They chatted about family matters for about twenty minutes. Mary could relax with her grandmother. Now that they were not involved in each other's lives she did not have to be constantly on guard. Previously, when they had all lived together in the same house, it had been different.

When the old lady said something about getting a cup of tea Mary said, "While you're putting the kettle on, Gran, I'm just going to stroll up to the top of the hill."

"Whatever for? You must have been up there thousands of times."

"I suppose that's why. I'll just go as far as the pine trees. I shan't be long."

"I shall never forget the day they carried you back. I can still see your little face. White and staring, you were. You looked as if you hated the whole world."

"I expect I did," Mary said. "I still do sometimes." Her own memories of the occasion were not so clear. "I'll only be a few minutes."

"Don't you go doing anything silly, now."

"Such as?"

"Well, climbing around in those old trees. Dry as tinder, they are."

"I'm a bit big for climbing trees," said Mary.

"Some people are never too old for silliness," the old lady grumbled. Mary made her escape and walked quickly up the lane to the top of the ridge.

When she reached the clump of pines she stood still for a moment, waiting. What she expected to happen wasn't at all clear to her, but as she had had this unexplained urge to stand at that point she certainly expected some sort of answer to emerge. In fact nothing did. She walked up and down on the lane where

Stephen had stopped the car. She picked up a small piece of broken glass from the shattered windshield. She stood looking down toward the river.

The faint sound of the gravel dredgers working in the flooded river came up to her. One or two lights began to appear in the windows of houses on the far side. She shivered, but not with any feeling of strange influences.

Nevertheless, before she went down the lane again she managed to identify what she believed to be the Conways' house. It stood back off the road running uphill away from the river. Quite a large house, protected from the weather and neighbors and traffic noise by shrubbery, but then of course the Conways were quite well off. Not rich like the Streeters but comfortable.

Stephen hadn't been at school this week. Margaret said they didn't know what was the matter with him. There was some strange story about his being asleep in a field. A couple of nuns had seen him. And now he didn't seem to know who he was. Mary went thoughtfully back down the lane toward the cottage. It was stupid to keep thinking about Stephen.

She spent another half an hour with her grandmother and then left to catch the bus home. At the end of the lane she hesitated. It was still early. Although the sun had set, there was still a thin wash of color in the sky and just the one bright planet following the sun down. She started to walk slowly and without conviction up the hill toward the Conways' house. She had covered about half the distance before she stopped.

"Blast!" she said aloud.

It relieved her feelings but solved none of her problems. Why shouldn't she go up to the house and ask how Stephen was if she felt like it?

The answer was obvious and immediate; because feeling like it wasn't enough. She thrust her hands downward in her cardigan pockets, dragging the garment even more out of shape, and stared moodily down into the gutter.

A car passed her going uphill. Its brake lights went on the moment it had passed and she looked up, thinking someone had recognized her and was stopping. It went sharp left, however, into the Conways' drive. She heard the door slam a few seconds later and the sound seemed to stimulate her to action. She swung away downhill and strode back the way she had come.

Almost immediately she found herself facing Margaret Conway coming uphill with a dog on a leash.

"Have you been to see Steve?" she said.

"No. As a matter of fact (as a matter of fact!) I've been visiting my aged grandparent. One or the other of us comes out every Wednesday."

"I've never seen you out here before. I don't know anyone named Silver around here. I thought I knew everyone."

"My mother's mother. Emmet."

"Old Mrs. Emmet? I know her. We're always running into her in the post office. She's a nice old duck. And she's got this gravelly voice—like Louis Armstrong— makes me go all tingly."

Mary grunted. She didn't really want to discuss her

79

grandmother. "How is Stephen?" she made herself ask.

"Hard to say. I think that was the doctor's car just went in. Why don't you come back with me and find out. Have you got to catch a bus or something?"

"There are plenty of buses, but . . ." Even with a direct invitation Mary didn't feel sure. "He won't want to see me if he's feeling rotten."

"My dear girl, he doesn't appear to recognize any of us. We can't get a word out of him. Just lies there with a sort of smug look on his face and eats everything that's put in front of him. Even tomatoes, which he usually hates."

"Well then . . ."

"No, come on. You never know. He might react to you. It's worth a try."

Mary allowed herself to be persuaded and the two girls walked on together. The doctor was already leaving as they came up to the front door. He was a youngish man who appeared to go everywhere in such a hurry that his unbuttoned jacket was always half a step behind him in the air. He smiled and gave a half-wave as he opened the car door.

"How is he?" Margaret asked, holding the edge of the door so that he couldn't slam it and leave.

"Much the same. But I've taken a good blood sample. We ought to get some information from that."

"Ghoul!" said Margaret and slammed the car door.

The doctor grinned and, spitting gravel, was gone.

"I wouldn't like my life to be in his hands," Margaret said as she waved Mary through into the front hall. "He's always in such a perishing hurry."

She hung up the dog's leash and started to go upstairs. "Come on," she said when Mary appeared to hesitate.

"Your mother . . ."

"Do you want to see her?"

"Not especially. I just thought—strangers wandering around the house—"

"You *have* been well brought up . . . no, it's not that sort of a house. Come on!"

Mary followed her up and then along a narrow passage that ran through to the back of the house. "Used to be the servant's bedroom in the old days. She even had her own bathroom—a slightly inferior one of course. Here we are."

She threw the door open and when she saw Mary hold back she went in first.

"Someone to see you, Steve!"

Stephen was sitting propped up against four or five pillows. His face had a sort of over-washed pallor but his eyes were bright and alert. His lips relaxed in the faintest suggestion of a smile.

Mary sat down on the chair by the bed. She couldn't think for a moment of anything to say and she glanced up at Margaret, who stood at the foot of the bed frowning at her brother.

"I'll leave you, then," she said. "Give a shout if you need anything. My room's on the right at the top of the stairs."

She pushed herself off the bed rail and moved toward the door.

"Blood," said Stephen.

Margaret came back. "Here, that's the first word I've

heard him speak since Sunday. Blood? I suppose it was that rotten doctor and his blood sample."

Stephen did not seem to notice her. He went on staring into Mary's face, only now he had an expression of concern. He had a handkerchief in his left hand. He folded it into a pad and then leaned forward, slowly reaching out until the pad was pressed firmly against the corner of Mary's eyebrow. He held it there for a few seconds, then withdrew it. He looked at the handkerchief and folded it. For a moment Mary thought she saw a stain of red on the white linen. She put one hand quickly to her forehead, but her fingers were unstained when she inspected them.

"Queer!" said Margaret. Then to her brother, "Steve! Did you see blood on her forehead? Did you think Mary's face was bleeding? No, it's no good. He's away again."

"Away?" said Mary.

"See for yourself."

Stephen's expression was now blank. His eyes were open but unfocused.

The two girls spoke to him but he did not react any more.

"For a moment, I thought . . ." began Mary. She reached out to take the handkerchief from Stephen's hand, but he clenched his fingers as if in anticipation.

Behind the blank expression and the unfocused eyes a silent struggle was in progress. Before him Stephen saw the long white bed, the two girls moving their mouths; he even knew who they were and what they were doing there. But he observed it as if through plate glass and with only a tiny part of his mind. At the same time he was aware of the smell of ransom plants and knew he was sitting by the side of the river looking across at a large wooden building.

Inside his head his own voice was speaking to him. "My name is Curwen," it said. "Who the devil is this Stephen?"

But it was the wooden building that engaged his attention. In the first place, the construction was ingenious. Perhaps a little too modern for conservative tastes, but pleasing nevertheless. The sides consisted of long, overlapping, wooden planks arranged horizontally and painted white. Half of the building hung out over the water.

Then he remembered. This was the new mill. Commune 417, or the New Vision Mill, as it was usually called. There'd been a great deal of talk when it was first built. It made use of the natural movement of the water to power the mill machinery.

His reverie was interrupted by the sound of voices and he saw that two people by the mill were shouting instructions to one another. One of these, a thin, fair-haired girl, was standing in a boat tied up just under the overhanging part of the mill. The other, a middle-aged man, his hair and face whitened with flour, was working a pulley at an open hatch halfway up the building. He was lowering a couple of bulging sacks down into the boat. Both wore commune blue, and when they had finished their task they looked up to see Curwen on the opposite bank.

"Can I come over?" he called.

"Where are you from?" asked the girl.

"Commune 84—the fish farm."

"I'm taking these down there later," she said. "There's room for you if you want to come."

"I'm not in a hurry," Stephen said.

"Do you want to see the mill first?"

"I've heard about it, of course. Some of the chaps came up when you first started. I always meant to. I'd like to see what goes on."

She took him over the mill, explaining as they went how the moving water of the river exerted a number of tiny pressures on the flat plates set around the circumference of the large water wheel and how these pressures added up to enough power to drive the simple milling machinery.

"The other improvement," she said, "is in the grinding stones themselves."

"Stones?"

"Yes, that's the point. Those small metal rollers in the steam-driven mills need a great deal of power. By using large flat stones we make use of inertia. Nothing could be more simple. And incidentally, everybody agrees that stone-ground flour has a much better flavor and is more nourishing."

"I hadn't noticed," Stephen said.

"You wouldn't have. Those two sacks in the boat are the farm's first order."

"Haven't you been down to the farm before, then?"

"Never."

"That's strange," said Stephen. "I've got this feeling we've met before."

The girl studied him carefully for a few seconds and then shook her head briefly. "No," she said. "I don't think so."

"Oh well."

They came out of the cool, dusty atmosphere of the mill and stood on the sun-warmed cobbles of the yard.

"We might as well go, then," the girl said. "Wait, though. I shan't be a minute."

She left him and ran into the rear part of the building, obviously the living quarters. Stephen waited awhile, then wandered over to where the boat was tied up. He undid the loop and held the end of the painter in his hand. It really was a fantastic spot, he thought, looking around. The clear cool water, just audible rustling by, the tall mature trees lining the farther bank, the splendid white mill building, the deep rumbling of the machinery —he turned slowly, admiring it all, taking long deep breaths and wondering why, just in this spot, the light should seem so magically golden. Everything it fell on seemed to glow inwardly.

The girl came running out of the house at that moment, calling something back over her shoulder. As someone called after her she half turned as if to hear better, stumbled on the cobbles, and sprawled.

Stephen hesitated, the end of the painter in his hand. Before he could reloop it the girl had jumped up again and was coming toward him, laughing and rubbing her arm.

"I didn't drop the bread," she said and held it out to him. "I thought you'd like to taste."

He took the small brown roll but hardly looked at it. His eyes were fixed on a tiny trickle of blood, deep red, that was creeping down her face from a small cut in her forehead. He found a handkerchief and pressed it on the cut. "Hold still," he said. "It'll clot in a minute."

But her eyes were fixed on him with dawning realization. "I do know you," she said. "You're Stephen Conway."

Mary looked at her watch. "I think I'll go. There's a bus in a few minutes."

They went downstairs without speaking. Mrs. Conway was crossing the hall, shuffling through some typewritten papers as she went. She was a thin, drawn woman with short graying hair. She wore a pair of heavy reading glasses with a chain looped around her neck.

"Mother!" said Margaret. "Stephen just spoke."

Mrs. Conway stopped. She took off her glasses and let them hang down in front of her. "Anything of moment?" she said.

"He said, 'blood.' "

"Blood?"

"Just one word, that's all."

"It was a dramatic word to choose," said Mrs. Conway. She did not appear to be making a joke.

"Oh, this is Mary Silver. I took her up to see Stephen. He seemed to recognize her. Well, at least he looked at her."

Mrs. Conway glanced at Mary and murmured something, probably a greeting. She put her glasses on again and looked down at the papers in her hand. "Oh Margaret," she said. "You know that punching machine for making holes in paper? I don't seem to be able to locate it."

"Sorry, I borrowed it," Margaret said. "I was straightening up my biology file. I'll fetch it for you in a minute. I'll just take Mary to the bus stop."

"Are you worried she may not be able to find it for herself?"

"That's hardly the point," said Margaret.

"I do wish you wouldn't take objects from my desk," said Mrs. Conway.

Margaret pressed her lips together tightly. She nodded at Mary and then toward the front door.

"Good night, Mrs. Conway," Mary said as she went out.

Mrs. Conway sat down on the bottom stair and started tapping the papers into a neat pack. She did not appear to hear. As they went out Margaret slammed the door.

"Childish," she admitted to Mary. "But it makes me feel better. Sorry about Mother. She can be quite pleasant when she puts herself out. Have you read any of her books?"

"No," Mary said. Then feeling that implied something that was not true, she added, "I didn't know she wrote."

"The anti-novel," said Margaret. "You know, people as objects. Very New Wave. She was mentioned on the Third Programme the other week. The bloke said she'd 'established a new austerity of vision' or something like that. Funny, really. What people don't realize is that Mother sees people like that anyway. The only good thing to be said about her is that although she sees us all as so many things, she doesn't try to manipulate us. She drives us mad, though, in other ways."

They reached the bus stop and stood waiting.

When the bus came Mary saw it was the same chatty conductor and decided to go to the upper deck.

Ten

The following afternoon Mary Silver went down to town to work in the public library.

The librarian said, "The issues for 1846 and '47 are all on microfilm. I'm sorry I can't let you use the actual files; they're in such a bad state."

"I don't mind using the projector," Mary said. "I've used it before."

"I know. It wasn't the projector itself I was thinking of. The trouble is, you see, we've had to move it temporarily into the basement. While the reference section is reorganized. You'll be among the reserve stock and the undisplayed stone axes, you see. And there's no heating . . . if you could leave it for a fortnight . . ."

"I've got this essay to write . . ."

"Well then, there's no help for it. I should keep your coat on if I were you."

Eventually Mary was installed in the basement, seated on an upturned box, in front of the microfilm projector.

Rough stacks filled with dusty, tattered books occupied most of the basement. The aisles were blocked with boxes and tea chests filled with everything from rusting militia helmets and stone-age artifacts to moth-eaten stuffed foxes bleached to an eerie yellow and blocks of ecclesiastical masonry. However, she was not likely to be disturbed, so she switched on the projector, opened her notebook, and decided to make the best of it.

For the next hour and a half she worked her way steadily through the two spools of microfilm. She was looking for reports of incidents connected in some way with the Poor Laws and she found enough to fill a dozen pages of her notebook. When she had reached the end of the second spool she was feeling quite exhausted and her eyes ached from the glare of the screen. She switched off and put her hands over her eyes to massage them and give them the relief of darkness for a while.

When she uncovered her eyes she saw that the screen was still glowing. She checked that the switch was in the off position. Thinking the switch to be broken, she pulled the plug out from its socket, but the screen remained lit.

"That's odd," she said aloud and inspected the screen itself.

What was appearing there was in fact a picture, rather like that to be seen on the closed-circuit television sets that operate in supermarkets. The picture it showed was of a shopping district or something like it, circular in shape and with the center occupied by a transparent dome-shaped structure. Various signs on the shops and on the transparent dome were in an alphabet Mary had never come across; a system of dots, almost a visible braille.

So far, she had only looked as one does at pictures of strange places, in a general sort of way. Now something about a figure seated at one of the tables set out in the open struck her as familiar. He looked exactly like Stephen Conway although he was dressed in a simple blue tunic with a fish motif embroidered on the front. It was amazing how like Stephen he looked.

Then, as he finished his drink and got up, he seemed even more like Stephen, for he moved like him. He went off out of sight to the right. The picture continued to show the district with its busy shoppers.

Mary gathered up her notebook and handbag, ready to leave, but found it difficult to drag herself away. Although the picture now showed her nothing of particular interest, its mere existence fascinated her. Only when she heard a sound on the stone stairs at the back of the basement was she able to wrench her eyes away.

The librarian himself was at the entrance, looking rather apologetic.

"How are you getting on down here?" he asked.

"I've finished. Thanks very much." She held out the two spools of microfilm.

"Did you find what you wanted?"

"Yes. It was very useful." Mary could not really concentrate on the matter. "Look," she burst out. "This projector—it's been doing some very odd things. . . ."

"Oh, I know," the librarian exclaimed, in a hurry to apologize. "Directly we finish our reorganization we're putting in much more modern equipment."

"No, I wasn't complaining. It worked perfectly well when I was using the film. But after I'd turned it off the screen stayed lit, and even when I pulled the plug out . . ."

"I'm hopeless with electrical apparatus," he said. "But they tell me there's a loose connection in the light source. I expect . . ."

Mary explained patiently that the machine had been switched off and unplugged and then went on to describe the scene she had been watching.

"Well, see for yourself," she said. "It's still there."

They went over to the projector, but the screen was dead. The librarian seemed a little uneasy. "That really is very strange," he said. "One of our assistants—Betty Arcoll—you may know her—was saying something very similar happened to her only a few days ago. I think she was teased a great deal as a result. You know what girls are. Anyway, no one took it very seriously. You ought to have a talk with her and and compare notes."

"I'd like to," Mary said. She glanced at her watch. "Actually it's later than I thought. . . ."

"If you don't seize the opportunity now," said the librarian with a smile, "you'll have to wait a very long time. Miss Arcoll is going off to take a course next week and this is her last day here with us. However, it's of no great consequence, I suppose. There's bound to be some perfectly obvious and simple explanation."

"There are more things in heaven and earth than are . . ."

"Oh I know, I know. People are always throwing that

little quotation about. But Hamlet wasn't being profound at that moment, was he? He was just being the Renaissance man poking fun at the stuffy 'philosophy' of the medievalists. . . . Oh dear, that was very rude of me, wasn't it? I have a didactic streak; I try to keep it under control but I'm not as successful as I should like to be. Most librarians are frustrated lecturers." He stopped suddenly in mid-flow, his lips parted for the next sentence, like an organ that has had the air cut off. "Miss Arcoll is working in the cataloging room if you'd like to see her," he added apologetically.

He led the way upstairs and showed Mary into a small room crowded with books piled untidily on every surface. "Betty," he said, "this young lady has had an Experience with the microfilm projector." Then he quickly withdrew and shut the door.

The girl sitting at the typewriter was very pretty in a cool, detached way. Her features were small and delicate and her skin had a bone-china quality. Her long dark hair hung forward over one shoulder. Her eyes were an unusual shade of green.

Eleven

Mary walked slowly and thoughtfully through the public gardens and out onto the old towpath. She couldn't think why she had come in this direction at all. The rear door of the library led out into the gardens and she had come out of the rear door, but that was no reason for continuing to walk in this direction. Her mother would be expecting her home to tea very soon.

She was still thinking about Betty Arcoll. The fact that they had both seen the same impossible picture was not half so surprising as Betty Arcoll's acceptance of it. This was not, she had said, by any means the first time. Quite often she had suddenly found herself looking through what seemed to be a window onto a different world.

Remembering the discussion at school, Mary had mentioned this and asked what Betty thought.

"I don't really understand all this math and space-time stuff," she had said. "I know it's real. At least, it's real for me. Just as the things you dream are real, when you're dreaming, anyway. It happens so often that I'm always ready for it nowadays.

"I remember once, when I was quite little, we went away to the seaside for a holiday and we stayed in a boardinghouse. I was in this strange bedroom—I always hated sleeping in strange bedrooms. Well, I was lying there, not feeling at all sleepy, and staring at the wallpaper. I can see it now, a whole mass of roses growing up a trellis which went on and on in all directions.

"Then I noticed that the paper was rubbed and worn in places, I don't mean torn, I mean worn through where something had rubbed against it, the edge of the mattress, for instance. And in those places you could see through the roses on their everlasting trellis to something quite different. It was a Chinese-willow-pattern sort of world underneath. I suppose now one would be conscious of the contrasting modes—the fake realism of the roses and the formal mannerisms of the equally fake Chinese. But then for some reason I was reassured and fell asleep quite happy.

"Well, that's what I feel about these odd breaks in the wall of everyday life. It's as if everything around us was rubbing a bit thin and something else was showing through. Do you see what I mean?"

Mary had left feeling very disturbed by it all. That girl had something queer about her; as if she herself was part of the something that was showing through. Uncomfortable and ill at ease, Mary had hurried away.

Although she could not explain why she was walking away from town along the old towpath, she continued along it. The river on her left ran with her, fairly deep at this point. Just ahead was the heavy stone embankment and the ruined buildings of what had once been the town wharf, hundreds of years before. Its use dated back to Roman times and the same site had been in use continuously until quite late in the nineteenth century. There had been talk of reviving it as a yacht base.

She was not actually thinking of this when she stepped onto the old wharf. In fact she was thinking that she really ought to turn around and go back. But for some reason she sauntered across the open paved space toward a long low building that had once been a warehouse. She went through the doorless arch and stood there for a few minutes letting her eyes get accustomed to the half-light. There was nothing to see except fallen tiles and rotting timbers. At the same moment she was filled with a sense of having accomplished what she set out to do. She swung around, feeling gay and a little excited.

Across the far side of the cobbled courtyard the boy from the fish farm was looping the boat's painter around the bollard. She ran out toward him. She felt her foot turn awkwardly and flung out an arm to save herself. She felt the sharp pain over her eye as her head struck stone but she scrambled to her feet immediately, still clutching the small whole-wheat roll she had returned to fetch. The boy was already halfway across the yard, looking concerned.

"There's a little blood—" he said and then reached out and pressed a folded handkerchief to her forehead. She saw the red stain on the linen before he doubled up the pad and put it away.

There was a moment during which they were both embarrassed, staring at each other and saying nothing, then Stephen gave an odd, self-conscious grin.

"I've just been having one of those creepy feelings," he said. "You know what I mean; when you think something has happened before, and you can almost—but not quite—tell what is going to happen next."

"That is odd, then. I had the same feeling, only in a very muddled, back-to-front way."

"You banged your head."

"Perhaps that accounts for it. Oh, here's the bread I was telling you about."

She tore the roll in two and gave him half. They munched in silence.

"Um," he said. "I see what you mean. Nutty. I like it."

They went over to the boat, still eating, and settled themselves in as best they could in the space left by the sacks. Mary fetched the boat around into the stream and then only used the paddle to keep on course, as the current was sufficiently strong to carry them down at brisk walking speed.

"You're not going to paddle back against this current, are you?" Stephen said after a while.

"No."

"I can't see any engine."

"There isn't one."

"All right, be mysterious."

Mary laughed and then leaned forward and began to operate a handle in the center of the boat. As she turned it a slender telescopic mast began to rise out of a small metal box amidships. When the mast had reached its full height a system of spokes rose out of it, umbrella fashion. Between the spokes were thin membranes which, as they were stretched, caught the wind which blew upriver. The boat checked in its course and began to swing around. Mary directed the boat's course with the paddle and in a few seconds they were moving steadily back upstream toward the mill.

"Convincing demonstration?" she asked.

"I'll say! It's marvelous." He studied the membranes. "They're like bats' wings."

"In fact it's supposed to be modeled on the wings of a butterfly emerging from its chrysalis. That handle operates a water pump. When you turn this the water is allowed to run out and—hey presto!"

The structure began to collapse and fold and a few seconds later had disappeared into its container. Mary swung the boat around again and they continued their journey downstream.

The movement and soft sound of the water, the steady but silent backward drift of the trees on either side, the warm sun filling the boat, all combined to discourage idle chatter. They half sat, half lay, moving through the quiet afternoon in silent companionship. This continued for five or ten minutes and then a truck went banging by on the road that ran alongside the river, raising dust and frightening birds.

"I was reading some old newspapers," Mary said. "More than a hundred years old, they were. Did you realize that in those days, with a population more than double what it is now, every single household in the country had its own transport? Many of them had two. They rushed around from place to place in continuous streams. Can you imagine the racket? And the smell? And so many of them were killed crashing into each other that the newspapers didn't even bother to mention it; they simply gave the number of those killed and injured at the end of each year. Isn't it sickening to think of?"

Stephen was lying back against the flour sacks with both hands behind his head and his eyes closed. "I can never really believe in the past. There's always something about it that doesn't ring true."

"But this wasn't a modern history book—this was an old newspaper, actually written and printed a hundred and something years ago. They weren't making it all up."

"I didn't mean that. I mean reality, or believability, or whatever you like to call it, is more to do with how you look at it than how it's pictured or described. Those newspapers may have described reality to those people who wrote and read them on that particular day. But to us they say something different. Because we're different. We think different thoughts, we have different preconceptions. When we read an old newspaper we see a world that never existed. It's even less real than a work of pure imagination, for that at least is entire and complete in one person's head."

There was quite a long silence—Stephen brooding, and Mary considering what he'd just said.

"Do you dream much?" she asked suddenly.

Stephen jerked up and stared at her, disturbed by this apparent irrelevance. "Dream? Everyone does. Or so they say."

"I mean remember what you've dreamed. Incorporate them into the world of daylight—that's what a sike said to me once."

"Oh. Well, yes, I do dream and yes, I do remember."

"When we met just back there you had this odd feeling of it all happening before. Was that to do with a dream?"

"No. Something quite different. Dreams are sharp and clear and the logic of the action—which seems okay when you're actually dreaming—makes no sense when you wake. The dream world is at a tangent to the waking world, if you see what I mean. But this other feeling is of something parallel. It could be going in the opposite direction but it's of the same nature as what's going on now."

"Like the image in a mirror?"

"Yes. I hadn't thought of it like that before. But it is."

"But the mirror world is everything reversed."

"Well, that's what I was talking about. The reality of your old newspapers . . . but let's think of something better . . . this progress bit. Everyone is concentrating madly on progress, aren't they? Your mill, this boat, and so on. We think of mankind making a sort of curve that approaches nearer and nearer to the natural straight line without ever actually touching it. We say that in the early history of mankind man was against nature—splitting atoms, wasting natural resources, and so on. Progress means coming around in this curve I was talking about, until now we only give our moral sanction to operations that coincide with the workings of natural forces, using sun, wind, water, temperature changes, rainfall, but not destroying or interfering. That's progress, isn't it?"

"You know it is."

"I don't know it is. I'm just living in a world that sees things that way. Suppose the reverse is true—the mirror image. Who says man is a natural part of nature? If we happened to live in a world going in the opposite direction we'd think of progress as going in the opposite direction too. We'd think steamboats were better than sailing boats and petrol-driven boats better still, and we'd think we'd really get somewhere if we invented a boat powered by splitting up atoms. We'd think speed was good and noise was good and crowds were good . . . there'd be no end to it."

"There would have to be an end," said Mary. "Going in that direction, you'd end by destroying the earth itself."

"But that's the point," said Stephen. "If you lived in a world that thought all these things were good, when it came to it you'd think destroying the world was good too. You'd probably think it was Good with a capital G. The ultimate. The final aim of mankind. The winning goal in a football match. Everyone would stand up and cheer as everything finally went up in smoke."

"It's terrifying," Mary said. "I'm glad all your sentences started with 'if.' "

"The trouble is," said Stephen, "I believe it does exist. I believe the two worlds lie side by side, both equally real. More than that, I believe I've seen through into the other side of the mirror. The odd thing is, I can't remember doing it and I don't know why I think it."

"I was talking to a girl today," said Mary, "who was saying something like that. She thought of patches rubbing thin so that you could see through—"

But as she said this a fit of cold shuddering seized her. She put both hands on the side of the boat and gripped tight. Beads of perspiration stood out on her forehead and she panted noisily, breathing through her open mouth.

"What's the matter?" Stephen said, leaning toward her. "Mary—"

She took a deep, sighing breath, recovering from the attack in a moment. "How did you know my name?" she asked.

"I was just wondering the same thing. I just knew it."

"And your name is Stephen."

"Yes. But I didn't tell you."

The boat had reached the first of the fish weirs and Mary had to concentrate on steering so as to bring them into the narrow bypass channel that ran in front of the commune buildings. She guided it into the side by the landing steps and Stephen jumped out with the painter.

"We're not so well organized as you are for handling heavy sacks," he said. "I'll go and get an able body or two."

Later, when the sacks had been unloaded, he helped her back up the channel, walking ahead with the painter while she fended off from the wall. Once in open water she began to pump up the mast.

"I'll come up to the mill tomorrow," Stephen said. "That is, if you don't mind."

"I don't mind," she said. Then she corrected herself. "Yes, I do mind. I'd like you to come."

Twelve

Stephen went up to the mill the following day after he had finished his work at the hatcheries. He found Mary already waiting for him, sitting out in the courtyard on a bench set against the white wooden wall. She was leaning back with her eyes closed and a faint smile on her lips, basking in the sun.

He went quietly, moving around her so as not to throw a shadow across her face. It occurred to him that he hadn't noticed before that her nose tilted up at the tip. He couldn't resist the temptation to touch it with the tip of one finger.

She didn't flinch or jump at his touch. Her eyes opened and the faint smile became more definite.

" 'Gat-toothed she was, and soothly for to say . . .' "

"That I am not," she said, jerking herself upright. She had reached up and taken his hand when he stroked her nose but now she threw it, rather as if it were a stone. Stephen allowed it to go on a limp arm and pretended to be dragged after it.

"And clowning won't help you," she added. "Gat-toothed is when you've gaps all the way around. Like a cat. Predatory. Which I am not."

"Show me your teeth. Come on—say cheese."

"Cheese—cheese—cheese!"

"There's definitely light showing between your two top incisors."

"And there's definitely a light showing in your eyes," she retorted. "The wickedness coming out, as my old grannie used to say."

Stephen laughed. "Wherever did you get that expression from?"

"What expression?"

"As my old grannie, etcetera—"

She looked absolutely stricken. "I did say that, didn't I? That's the second time."

"The second time you've suddenly produced an old grannie? Incidentally, what is a grannie? Some sort of blood relative, isn't it?"

"I meant it's the second time I've found myself saying something that seemed to have got into my head from somewhere else—if you see what I mean?"

"It's probably your past inclinations catching up with you."

"You're not taking it very seriously, are you?"

"No," he said. "I'm not. I want to walk by the river."

She smiled and nodded and they moved off side by side down the pathway. For the first few yards it was a worn path, part of the mill grounds, but when they reached the first bend in the river the path was more overgrown with the lush waterside growth of yellow irises and tangled figwort.

Mary dropped back half a step. "It's too narrow," she said.

"Not if we walk closer," he said and put his arm around her shoulders to demonstrate.

For a fraction of a second she stiffened but as quickly she relaxed, laughed, and put her arm around behind him and hooked a thumb in his belt. "And walk in step," she added as they bumped hips.

"You're quite different today, aren't you?" she said when they had walked some way in rhythmical silence. "Yesterday you were doom-laden and prophetic and a bit worrying. I thought a lot about what you said last night. It disturbed me, and yet I couldn't quite tell why."

"That's me," Stephen. "Flashes of brilliant non-sense. That's what my tutor wrote on my final report."

Mary refused to be sidetracked. "But today," she went on seriously, watching their feet moving in unison, "you're bubbling about all over the place. What's happened?"

"It's the effect you have on me," he said, but lightly, so as not to disturb her.

"Empty-headed female?"

"No!"

He stopped abruptly and swung her around so that they were facing each other—close, serious, and intent. She could feel his arm hard across her shoulder. "You know I didn't mean that."

She squeezed his waist quickly, lightly, then laughed and moved on, so that he was forced to fall into step again. "Of course not. I was joking." Nevertheless, the sudden intensity made her feel quite dizzy for a moment.

105

They had come to an open space on a small promontory where a large red-gum had half fallen over in the damp soil. One branch lay on the ground.

"Let's sit a minute," she said and, disengaging herself, sat on the low branch.

Stephen looked up into the top of the tree. Then he leaped at a branch, pulled himself up, and swung over until he was hanging by his toes, his upside-down face only a few feet from hers. "Can you do this?" he said in a rather thick voice.

"Show-off!"

"But can you?"

"I've got a thing about trees," she said. "I haven't climbed trees since I broke my leg at the age of—"

She jumped to her feet and went quickly to the bank of the river. There she stood for a few minutes, pressing her hands together, staring at the moving water.

"At the age of what?" asked Stephen, still inverted on his branch. "Are thin people always nervy?"

She did not appear to hear him. He watched the movement of her shoulder blades for a moment, then unhooked himself and dropped to the ground. He went over and stood close behind her, not sure how to behave. Her hair had a warm, scorched smell, like toast almost. "What is it?" he said quietly and put one hand lightly on her shoulder.

She twisted around suddenly and pressed herself close to him with her face hidden in his shoulder. "I'm frightened," she cried. "It's like being invaded. I don't know which is me!"

Stephen stroked her hair and waited. The strands

106

were so pale and fine that the sunlight made small, flashing spectra among them. She raised her head suddenly and looked at him. "Do you know what I'm talking about?" she asked. He shook his head. Her breath was hot and damp. He gently removed tears from each eye with the tip of his little finger.

"Thanks," she said and laughed and then gave her head a quick shake. "Oh—I don't know. I can't explain it, really. I already told you—I keep saying things and when I hear them coming out it's like listening to someone else. Where do the words come from? I don't think them. They come by themselves. But how can they? Where do they come from?"

He had no explanation and said nothing.

"I just said that about not climbing trees—well, I never did break any legs or anything. I haven't got a thing about trees. Then what made me say I had? Do you think I'm going off my head?"

"Of course not."

"There's no of course about it. People do. I've often wondered what it felt like. Inside, I mean. Well, if it's like this I'm sorry for them. It's terrifying, not being in control."

They walked on along the riverbank. Stephen tried to help, tried to be reassuring. He dug into his memory for anything he had read about the unconscious mind, about dreams, repressed desires, and so on.

She interrupted him abruptly. "It's no use. Look, you were saying much the same thing yourself yesterday."

"I was?"

"You were talking about parallel existences—"

"Yes, but that wasn't on a personal level. I was thinking of the whole of society."

"It would still have to be on a personal level in the end, wouldn't it? Suppose it's not parallel societies but parallel personalities?"

"Everybody schizoid?"

"Why not? You were talking about progress; perhaps that's real progress. The unwinding of the strands. All the psychology I've ever read has been concerned about the double nature of the mind; conscious and unconscious, the dark and the light side. Even in religion it's always gods and devils. Perhaps we're getting to a point where the tangle can be unraveled. We'll all turn into discrete pairs. No more confusion."

Stephen glanced sideways at her, worried. There was a strong note of hysteria in her voice and he saw that her cheeks were flushed and her eyes unnaturally bright.

"That's just words," he said. "Doesn't mean anything."

She stopped suddenly and turned around. "I want to go back to the mill," she said in a firm, normal voice.

Stephen thought it must have been the way he had spoken. "I'm sorry," he said. "I didn't mean—"

"No," she said. "No, it wasn't you. A cold hand was suddenly removed. It went, that's all. I was being silly."

He didn't like to argue, although he felt there was more to it than that. They fell into step again. She took his hand and bent her arm up inside his.

"All the same," she said thoughtfully a few minutes later, "something's going on."

"Someone was telling me about toadstools," Stephen said.

"Said he, changing the subject."

"No, I'm not changing the subject. Apparently in the old days people used to press the juice out of those bright red toadstools and take the extract as a sort of drug. Did you know?"

"No."

"Well, the idea is that all those old prophets and soothsayers and oracles and what-have-you were really people who'd taken an overdose. How does that get you?"

"That's just an elaborate way of saying, 'Perhaps it's something you've eaten,' isn't it?"

"Oh, I suppose so. Still, it's interesting."

They walked on. Stephen noticed that they were no longer strolling, but that Mary was forcing the pace. "What's all the rush?" he asked eventually.

"I have this feeling I ought to get back."

"Do you have to?"

"Not really. I just have the feeling. Do you mind?"

"Well, of course I mind. But I'll put up with it."

"I don't want you to go," she said. "It's just getting back that seems important."

"Perhaps the mill's on fire. Premonitions and all that."

"Don't say that."

"I already have. But I wasn't serious."

"You could come in with me. I'd like you to meet the others. We're a very small group, you know. Not like your gigantic enterprise. It doesn't take many people to grind grain."

"The question is, would they like to meet me?"

"Anyone would like to meet you."

"Flattery will get you nowhere."

They went on, making stupid jokes, laughing, almost back to the gaiety of an hour before. They reached the mill courtyard and were halfway across it when Stephen happened to glance up at the doorway. With his silly joke about a fire still in his mind, he stopped abruptly and gaped at the doorway. Mary looked up quickly. He heard her make a strange moaning sound.

"What's happened?" he cried.

They went slowly closer. The neat doorway in the white-painted wall had gone and in its place was a doorless hole giving onto darkness and desolation.

Mary broke away from him and ran forward.

"Don't go in there!" he shouted, but as she did not stop he followed. She went out of the sunlight and into the dark opening and at the same moment seemed to be extinguished.

"Mary!" he shouted and hesitated before following her through. He entered the mill kitchen, shining and scrubbed, with two men seated at the long wooden table. They looked up at him curiously.

Thirteen

It took him some moments to compose himself. "Sorry," he said. "I was . . . I thought . . ."

The two men continued to look at him, waiting. They were both stolid-seeming, middle-aged men, not much given to showing extremes of emotion. At the moment they seemed to be exhibiting a mild curiosity.

"You seem to be in a bit of a state," said one of them. "Sit down for a minute if you like."

"Thanks. I . . . I was looking for Mary." He was still bewildered by the sudden change of scene. "I thought she came in here."

The man who'd spoken first shook his head. "She didn't, though."

"We were walking across the courtyard together just now, and then all at once . . ."

"We saw you in the courtyard," said the second man. "We saw you come all the way across, talking and laughing to yourself, you were." He pointed through the open door and Stephen saw that indeed the whole court-yard lay within their view. "Then you shouted some-thing and came toiling in here like a mad dog was at your heels. That's about right, isn't it?" he added to the other man.

"That's about the size of it."

Stephen laughed, self-conscious rather than amused, and passed a hand across his eyes. The two men seemed like caricatures rather than real people. He could not take them seriously enough to explain to them what he thought had happened. "I must have been dream-ing," he said. "I'm very sorry—rushing in on you like that."

"You're welcome."

He smiled apologetically and backed out through the doorway, waiting for the moment when the scene would change again and both men disappear. It re-mained solidly the same, however, even when he had backed farther than made sense. Realizing how ridicu-lous he must appear in their eyes, he turned quickly away and walked toward the river. He thought he heard one man say to the other, "If that's not a case for the sikes I'm a Ditlander!"

He hurried along the riverbank, back in the direc-tion of the fish ponds. Was he a case for the sikes? Was it as simple as that? Perhaps there was no such person as Mary and he had been talking to himself—his other half?—all the afternoon. It certainly explained her be-havior—or apparent behavior—if it was in fact all part of something going on in his own head.

He tramped on, going over the incidents of the afternoon one by one, making them fit a new pattern. And yet, he thought in the midst of it, if I can do this coolly and calmly then there can't be anything wrong. Unless to be cool and calm about one's own sanity was itself a sign of the disturbed mind.

When he reached the farm he felt thirsty and went first into the common room where, at this time of the day, the bar would be open. He heard the laughing and talking while he was still on the steps outside and felt reassured; that was a familiar and real enough sound in any case. He even smiled slightly to himself as he identified the big-bear bass of the farm director telling what was obviously an amusing story.

But as he stepped though the doorway the laughter suddenly died out. He looked across sharply to the big circular table at the far end of the room. The farm director and half a dozen commune workers were seated around it with their glasses on the table before them. They had all turned to look at him.

As he stared back they turned away one by one and started a murmured conversation. The farm director sat up straighter and called out in a more than usually hearty voice, "How are you feeling now, Curwen?"

"All right," he said, surprised.

"Glad to hear it," he said, and then turned immediately back to his audience. "Well, as I was saying, he was trying to keep hold of this big carp with one hand. . . ."

Stephen went up to the bar and asked for a large ale.

The duty barman was Orin. He looked uneasy. "A large one?" he said rather louder than necessary, and as he said it he glanced across toward the big table.

Stephen turned quickly and was just in time to catch the farm director's nod.

"What's the matter?" he demanded. "Is it rationed or something?"

"Rationed?" said Orin. "Course not. I just wondered, that's all."

"Wondered what?" Stephen was by now thoroughly on edge.

"A chap can wonder, can't he?" said Orin mildly. "It's a free country."

"You must want something to wonder at if a large ale sets you going." Stephen raised the glass and took a long drink. As he lowered it he saw Orin looking at him rather oddly. "Well?" he said.

"It's not like you to sink three straight off, that's all," said Orin apologetically.

"Three? You must be joking. I've only just come in, haven't I?"

"If you say so."

"If I say so? What sort of an answer is that?"

"Oh, don't take any notice of me. I've had a trying day," said Orin and gave an embarrassed sort of grin.

Stephen studied him more closely. "You've got a nasty bruise coming up on your cheek," he commented. "How did you come by that?"

"Well, if that doesn't take the . . ." Orin seemed about to explode, then he suddenly controlled himself and, muttering something about having glasses to wash, disappeared into the back room.

Stephen took his glass to one of the smaller tables and sat down thoughtfully. "Now careful!" he warned himself. "It's probably you that's being odd, not them. Take it easy."

There was no doubt that everybody in the room was shooting very odd glances at him from time to time. He sat sipping the remainder of his drink, sulking a little, feeling put upon, and then, feeling weary of the whole business, he decided to go to bed. He took his empty glass back to the bar and as he did so the farm director stood up and walked over toward him.

"Why don't you turn in and have an early night," he said, putting one hand on Stephen's shoulder in a friendly way.

Stephen detected something odd in his tone but again, turning his gaze inward, realized the oddness might be in his head and so he forced a smile.

"I was thinking of doing just that," he said. "It's been a queer sort of afternoon."

"Not quite the word I should have used." The director patted Stephen's shoulder a couple of times. "You don't have to go rushing down to the hatcheries in the morning. See how you feel first."

Stephen didn't answer. He walked slowly across the courtyard toward the dorm, trailing one hand over the glossy leaves of the potted plants. He picked a petal and held it between his lips, enjoying the silky texture. Why had the director been so concerned about him? It was almost as if he had been there at the mill and seen it all. Otherwise how could he know? Perhaps those two at the mill had contacted him; the fish emblem on his tunic would have told them where he came from.

He entered the dorm and went toward his own bed,

not noticing until he was right up to it that it was already occupied. At the other end of the dorm Wint was bending down by his bed sorting papers out of a box onto the top of the bed. He glanced up at Stephen, grunted something, and then went on with what he was doing.

"There's someone in my bed!" exclaimed Stephen. "What goes on?"

Wint straightened up and looked across with his usual slightly amused expression and then his face changed quickly. "Hey, I thought . . ." He came forward a couple of paces and then stopped again, obviously in doubt.

"You thought what?"

Wint shook his head as if he'd rather not say and switched his eyes back to the occupied bed.

"Well, whoever he is, he can't have my bed," said Stephen and twitched the covers back.

The trespasser groaned and rolled over. The face that stared back at Stephen from the pillow was his own. For a moment the usurper blinked and stared, then he threw the covers off and leaped out of the bed.

"What the hell goes on?" he exclaimed.

For a moment they stood staring at each other, crouched, ready, like two dogs about to fight. Then Stephen backed slowly away, holding both hands up in front of him as if to blot out the other's face.

"Hang on a minute!" cried Wint anxiously. "I'll fetch the . . ."

But Stephen didn't wait. He turned and stumbled toward the door. Wint followed and caught up with him in the courtyard. He grasped his arm. "Curwen! Wait a minute! Don't do anything silly!"

"I'm not Curwen," muttered Stephen, trying to shake Wint off. "That's him. You can see for yourself. Let me go." He crossed the courtyard, dragging Wint along with him.

"Where will you go? Let me get help, Curwen! We can sort this out. It's some silly mistake."

"I'm going back to the mill," Stephen said. His mind was in a turmoil but somewhere at the back of his thoughts was the idea—feeling—that whatever happened to Mary when she went through that eroded doorway ought to have happened to him also. If he went back there perhaps it would all straighten out.

Wint trotted beside him still holding his arm, although Stephen was doing his best to shake free. He kept arguing, holding him. The noise they were making must have penetrated to the common room, for the director and two others suddenly appeared at the corner of the yard.

Wint appealed to them and they quickly came over. Stephen stood in the midst of them panting. He tried to struggle but they held him securely, so he gave up and merely repeated, "I must get back to the mill. I must. Let me go. I've got to get back there before it's too late."

He heard the conversation going on around him in a jumble of sounds from which now and then a sentence, or part of one, seemed to emerge like a clear shape rising through muddy water.

"No, two of them, I'm telling you—"

"One of you go and—"

"—not impossible. There was a case, many—"

"Curwen! Can you hear? We're taking you to—"

"Surely he can walk by himself."

"—gone wooden—"

"We don't know enough about—"

"Must get him to the sikes."

It was like finding the right key after trying dozens of wrong ones. Stephen felt himself relax, fall away, flow like water. He knew he was being carried. He felt he was thinning out, dispersing, like a mist that the sun shines on. He was airily pleased with himself for behaving so properly. "Five," he said to himself in the fading shadows of his mind.

Four.

Three.

Two.

One.

Zero.

Fourteen

Mary stood looking at the broken tiles, the rubbish pushed back into corners, the wetness. It smelled of fungus and decay. She shuddered and turned to leave. For a fraction of a second she had a sensation that something desirable was outside. She even saw herself going, as it were, in advance of herself, already a few paces outside the doorway and in sunshine. But the feeling left her before it had become definite. She went thoughtfully out and began to walk up the riverbank toward the town.

It was gray and overcast, a somber, chilling sort of day, not actually raining but with large drops of moisture dripping from the trees. A bus, going by on the other bank where the road was, had its inside lights on. Tires made diminishing wet sounds on the surface of the road.

She wasn't dressed for such weather and she found she could not recall what it had been like when she came out. When she brushed her hand down her cardigan it left her palm running with moisture. She put her head down and hurried. It would take her at least half an hour to get home. She concentrated on getting there as quickly as possible.

Some time later the sound of another vehicle coming along the road broke through her concentration. Another bus so soon? She glanced up and saw that in fact it was an ambulance with light flashing, but siren silent. Urgent but not an emergency. As it drew level and then drew on out of sight she suddenly had an absolute conviction that Stephen was in it. She just knew.

She was so sure that ten minutes later as she reached the edge of town and passed a telephone booth she stopped and rang the Conways' number. Margaret answered.

"About Stephen," said Mary, omitting all introductory chat.

"That's Mary, isn't it? How did you know? They've just taken him."

"Taken him where?"

"To the hospital. Oh, I'm sorry, did you think . . . ? Well, it's bad enough, I suppose. He went into a coma. They still don't have the faintest idea what's wrong but they said he had to be in the hospital to be looked after properly. Are you still there?"

"Yes."

"How did you know?"

"I saw an ambulance and felt sure he was in it."

"How queer. I mean you see so many ambulances. . . ."

Mary didn't want to discuss this. "Who went in with him? Was it your mother?"

"Well, no. Actually Mother's going to Paris tomorrow for a conference and she was too busy packing. No, in fact no one went in with him. What was the point? He was just lying there like a log. . . ."

"Good-bye," said Mary and hung up. "Conference in Paris!" she said to the smeared mirror behind the phone. "Big deal!"

As she walked, she considered going straight up to the hospital but finally decided to go home first and change and then find out about visiting hours. She strode grimly through the wet streets in a black and savage mood toward her home.

She let herself in the back way and began peeling off her wet cardigan as she went through the kitchen. At the foot of the stairs she paused to look into the front room where she could hear the whirring of the Hoover. Her mother had her back to the door; obviously she had not heard the door open. Mary went on upstairs.

In her bedroom she stripped off her wet clothes, dried her face and hair, and then put on jeans and her favorite turtle-necked jersey. As she was combing her hair at the mirror she glanced at the clock on her dressing table and was surprised to see that it showed just after ten o'clock. How could it be ten o'clock? It was broad daylight. She could see by the sweep-second hand that the clock was going. Puzzled a little, she switched on her transistor for a time check and started hunting under her bed for another pair of shoes. She was still on her hands and knees when she heard her mother's voice from the bottom of the stairs.

"Who's up there?" The voice was strained and anxious.

"Me, of course," Mary said. She dragged the shoes out

and sat on the edge of the bed to put them on. Her mother's feet came clattering up the stairs.

"My God! It *is* you. What a turn you gave me." Mrs. Silver was leaning against the side of the door, panting, staring at Mary as if she were seeing a ghost.

"For goodness' sake," said Mary impatiently. "Who else would it be?" She stood up and started hunting in the wardrobe for her raincoat.

"You're a cool one and no mistake. You just walk in as if nothing had happened. . . ."

"And I'm just walking out again in a minute," said Mary. "They've taken Stephen Conway to the hospital, so I'm going up there to visit him."

"You're doing no such thing," exclaimed Mrs. Silver. "Not until I've had an explanation."

"What have I got to explain now?" demanded Mary. "You're always asking me to explain, and when I do, you don't even listen."

"There's no need to be rude. We may not all be as clever as you. . . ."

"Oh, Mum!"

"Look, my girl, you may think you can go out when you like, come in when you like, go off entirely for two days without saying a word to anyone—but that's because you've got no feelings for other people. What do you think I've felt, not even knowing where my own daughter's gone to. And all the trouble it's caused other people. What about the police for a start. . . ."

"Stop, Mum! Wait a minute!" Mary sat back on her bed with a bewildered expression. "Are you trying to tell me I've been out of this house for two days?"

"Well, you know you have. It doesn't need me to tell you that. What I want to know is, what have you been doing?"

"But I haven't . . . Mum, listen. I went out for a walk along the river. I went as far as the old Roman wharf and then I turned back. I can't have been more than a couple of hours at the most."

Mrs. Silver made a snorting noise to show what she felt about the truth of this statement.

"How can I have been out for two days?" said Mary. "I'd remember something about it, wouldn't I?"

"Well, I've been at my wit's end, I can tell you. The police found someone who saw you walking by the river the night before last. And after that—nothing. Of course it was clear enough what the police thought. Especially as you were seen by the river. . . ."

"Mum! Stop it! I don't know what you're talking about."

Mrs. Silver looked at her daughter for some moments. She had a shrewd, calculating look on her face. She did not seem disturbed by Mary's obvious distress. In fact it was clear she thought Mary was putting on a performance.

"You can save your energy," she said sourly at last. "It won't wash with me, you know. You've been up to something, my girl, something you don't want me to know about. But it'll all come out in the end, you see if it doesn't."

"I haven't done anything. I don't know what you're talking about."

"If you expect me to believe you've been wandering

around the best part of two days suffering from loss of memory, you've got another think coming. Someone would have seen you, wouldn't they?"

Mary was too muddled and bewildered to think of it sensibly. She didn't really believe her mother, who seemed to be talking hysterically and at random. Perhaps her mother was on the point of a nervous breakdown. It wouldn't be the first time. There was that dreadful time about ten years before—Mary could not remember the details, only how frightened she'd been —when her mother had been taken away for a long time, two or three months anyway. Her father had denied all the tales the neighbors were telling about how Mrs. Silver had tried to set the house on fire and harm her own child. "She's gone away for a much-needed rest," was all he'd say. "She's been overdoing things."

"You're not listening to a word I've said," Mrs. Silver said sharply.

"I was trying to think."

"Well, you'll need to think up a better story than that."

"I'm not thinking up any story!" Mary replied angrily. "You're the one who's doing that. I keep telling you, nothing happened. Nothing! Nothing!"

"So you went for a walk. Came back two hours later. And anybody who thinks different is either mad or lying. That's it, is it?"

"I know what I did," said Mary sullenly.

"All right then. What time did you go out?"

"I was working in the library . . ." She suddenly recalled the odd occurrence with the microfilm projector and began to feel uneasy. "I had a talk with a girl there called Betty Arcoll and then I came out through the gardens. And then for some reason I thought I'd go along the river for a walk before coming home to tea. I suppose it must have been about half past four."

"I see." Mrs. Silver was already smiling in a smug, triumphant sort of way. "So by your reckoning it ought to be about half past six now. Have you seen the clock?"

"I thought it must have stopped."

"No, the clock's not the one that's mixed up. See, it says nearly half past ten."

"I must have been a bit longer than I thought. I suppose I must have been thinking and not noticed."

"But it's half past ten in the morning!" cried Mrs. Silver thoroughly exasperated. "In the morning! And not even the next morning!"

Mary stared at her mother, hating her for forcing her to accept this impossible disconnection. Then she threw herself back on her bed and covered her face. "Go away," she said. "Leave me alone and let me think. I've got to try to remember."

"All you've got to do is to tell the truth," said Mrs. Silver. "I'll never understand why you find it so hard." Then, having won, she could be generous. "I expect you'll be hungry," she said. "I'll go and fix you a snack."

Mary didn't move or speak. She lay straight out on her bed, her hands covering her face. She took long, deep, regular breaths, trying to control something very close to panic that she felt rising within her.

"I shan't be long," said Mrs. Silver and went downstairs.

125

Central Jr. High School Library

As soon as she was alone Mary took her hands from her face and, after stretching slowly and luxuriously, put them behind her head. She stared down the long landscape of herself to her feet and crossed ankles. Like a crusader on his tomb.

For a while she thought about the simple, unified life of a crusader; a simple aim carried out by simple physical action. Then she remembered the Templars. They hadn't found it so simple. Easy to say, "Drive the infidel out of Jerusalem," but what happened when you found that there was more to admire in the infidel's faith and way of life than in your own? Then you were truly in a dilemma. "O! now, for ever Farewell the tranquil mind; farewell content! Farewell the plumed troop and the big wars that make ambition virtue!" Who said that? Othello of course. "Othello's occupation's gone!"

But why, for goodness' sake, was she thinking about crusaders? She had intended to search for two missing days. It was no use. The two days would have to search for themselves; she no longer felt interested.

She sat up and, propping her back against the head of the bed, stared at her reflection in the long wardrobe mirror. If only the mirror could show her something else. Like Beauty seeing the Beast dying for love of her. Or the Lady of Shalott seeing "an abbot on an ambling pad"—no—seeing that other crusader Sir Lancelot, with his "gemmy bridle glittering free."

"And that," she thought, "is the oddest story of them all. One world going on outside—market girls, abbots, and knights, and what-have-you—and she inside, seeing it only through a mirror."

Suddenly she jumped off the bed. " 'The mirror crack'd from side to side,' " she said. "Of course. And so did the windshield. I must go and tell him about the Lady of Shalott."

She snatched up her raincoat and ran to the stairs. Her mother was already halfway up with a tray.

"Where do you think you're off to, then?"

"I must go out."

"Oh yes?"

"Stephen Conway's in the hospital. I'm going to see him. I've got to tell him about . . ."

"About what?"

"Oh, just things. School things."

"If he's in the hospital I don't suppose he'll be that interested. And anyway his family will be visiting. You can't just barge in. Apart from which," she concluded, "visiting hours are not in the morning."

"I expect they'll let me see him." Mary had waited for her mother to reach the top of the stairs. Now she tried to push past.

"I made an omelette for you. Bacon omelette. Specially for you."

"I'm not hungry."

"You must be. You can't go two days without eating."

"How do you know I haven't been eating?"

"Ah! Now we're coming to it, aren't we?"

"We're not coming to anything. I just meant I don't know any more than you do. I wish you'd just leave me alone."

Mrs. Silver looked as if she was going to snap angrily

back but then she stopped herself, seemed to shrink somehow, and turned away with the tray to go back downstairs. Mary felt as if she had killed something.

"Oh, Mum!" she exclaimed. "Don't. Why do we always fight each other? I'd love to eat it. Really I would."

Her mother responded so quickly, came back up the stairs so eagerly, so vulnerably, that Mary felt even worse. Why did people have to be so fragile?

She sat down on her bed with the tray beside her and began to eat. She found she was in fact quite hungry. Mrs. Silver moved around the room, shutting the door of the wardrobe, closing a drawer, picking up wet garments off the floor. "You got yourself soaked," she commented.

"It began to rain suddenly."

"It's been raining steadily since yesterday morning."

Mary took in this piece of information but did not comment on it. Instead she said, "Did you really have the police looking for me?"

"I said so, didn't I?"

"I thought you might just be getting at me."

"They didn't take it all that seriously," Mrs. Silver admitted. "The sergeant said they had more teenage girls reported missing than I'd had hot dinners, and they all turned up a couple of days later."

"You said that about the river though."

"Well, I was stretching it a bit then. You made me cross."

"I'll call in at the police station as I go up to the hospital. It's on the way."

"Are you serious about this Conway boy?"

"What on earth do you mean by that?"

"You know well enough."

"I could make an inspired guess. It would be a lot easier if you said what you meant."

"Well, I think," said Mrs. Silver, raising her voice a little as if she were shouting across the chasm between them, "that you ought to save that sort of thing until after you've taken your exams."

"What sort of thing?"

"Getting involved."

"Involved with people? We all do that all the time, don't we? No man is an island."

"It's like banging your head against a brick wall," exclaimed Mrs. Silver in a defeated voice. "I'll take the tray down if you're finished."

Mary waited for her mother to get well out of the way before she left. As always after these pointless exchanges she felt a mixture of guiltiness and smug self-satisfaction, followed by a wave of disgust and disapproval. She sat for a while considering her own inexcusable behavior, then she snatched up her raincoat and paused to scowl at herself in the long mirror.

"Stop wallowing!" she ordered her reflection.

The rain had stopped and the sky was being cleared by a very resolute wind.

The policeman at the inquiries desk was young and relaxed. He did not ask Mary for any explanatory details. When he had made a note of what she told him in a long narrow ledger he said cheerfully, "Another major crime solved," and shut the book with a snap. Mary laughed and that was all there was to it.

The porter at the hospital had no record of Stephen being admitted. "Been a proper muddle here all day," he complained. "Half the staff are working strictly by the rules because of some wage dispute. The other half don't know whether they're coming or going."

"So he might be here?"

"There were two or three empty carts down the passage there about an hour ago. I don't know where the patients went to. Discharged themselves, probably —sick of waiting about. I tell you it's a proper shambles here."

Mary decided to look for herself and began to wander through a maze of corridors, peeping into each room she came to. No one stopped her but she got some very curious looks. At one point she found herself in a rather smelly yard entirely surrounded by dustbins and was about to turn back into the building when she happened to glance over the low box-hedge that was intended to screen this area from passersby. About a hundred yards down the road leading away from the back entrance a familiar figure was doing a jog-trot toward the gate. She scrambled through the hedge and chased after him.

"You're supposed to be in a coma," she panted, coming level.

Stephen stopped and looked at her with amazement. "I was just thinking about you," he said. "At least, I think I was. I had this dream, you see. If it was a dream. . . ."

"Go on!"

"I must tell you about it before I forget the details."

"Shouldn't you be in there, having care and attention?" She jerked her thumb back in the direction of the hospital.

"I feel splendid. Let's forget the hospital and go down and have a coffee in the Fanfare. I must get it off my chest."

Fifteen

$$T$$hey sat for a long time over their empty coffee cups. "Do you want to get away? Go home to lunch or something?" he asked.

"No. Go on with what you were saying."

Stephen told her about his dreams. What he remembered of them was a series of fragments but they made some sort of continuous sense: the fish commune, the center, the cloisters.

"The cloisters?"

"Yes. Odd, that. The cloisters were exactly the same. The only parts of the dream that were, come to think of it. And some of the people. Myself, although I seemed to have a different name. I can't remember what it was. And you."

"Me?"

"Yes, you were there." He began to tell her about the mill and as he did so she was seized with a fit of shivering. "Are you all right?" he asked.

"A bit frightened."

"I don't get it."

"According to my mother I've been missing for nearly two days. I can't remember anything. Except that I walked down to the old wharf and back."

"But that's exactly where this mill would have been! Good grief!"

"Can one person break through into another's dream? I mean really break through?"

"It doesn't make sense, does it? Dreams are in your head. You can't disappear for two days into someone else's head. I mean, a dream isn't something tangible, a thing. It's a sort of pattern that occurs in your head."

"People didn't always think so. What about shape-changing?"

"But that's superstitious nonsense, isn't it?"

"Of course."

They sat for a long time without saying anything.

"I feel . . ." she said suddenly.

"The odd thing . . ." Stephen burst out at the same moment. They both laughed. "You go on," Stephen said.

"It was only . . . well, sometimes thoughts come clearer if you say them aloud."

"So?"

"I was thinking of this feeling I have of being pushed and pulled about. Of being powerless. I mean, it seems as if I'm . . . both of us perhaps . . . we're being dragged backward and forward through some wretched hole. I mean, if there really are two worlds coinciding in time and place there ought not to be a hole between them at all."

"There seem to be dozens of holes."

133

"But only for us. Why us? I don't like being a puppet. I'd like to choose . . . this side or the other."

"I think we are choosing," Stephen said. "Then it makes more sense. We keep changing our minds—or not making them up firmly. I think if we were quite positive about what we wanted, then it would all stop. We'd be on one side or the other."

"Permanently?"

"I suppose so."

She thought about this. "That's rather frightening."

Stephen looked into his empty cup, then put it down again. "I suppose we ought to be going."

"Yes."

They went slowly down the steps to the shopping area below and walked slowly, side by side, the length of the pavement. Pigeons scattered under their feet to let them through. They both felt reluctant to separate.

"You were going to say something," Mary said.

"Was I? When?" He knew very well what she meant.

"Earlier. When I interrupted."

"Oh, that! Just an observation."

"About what?"

They reached the end of the shopping area. Here they needed to turn—one left, the other right—to go their separate ways. Stephen frowned at the traffic as he spoke. "I was going to observe that you and I appeared to be . . . well, much more friendly through there," he waved vaguely, "than we usually are here." He had put it stupidly but it would have to do.

"Yes," she said. "Although . . ."

He didn't prompt her and she did not say the rest of

what she was thinking.

"I suppose we ought to be at school," he said in a more casual voice. He felt a load had been lifted.

"I certainly ought to be. But you are supposed to be lying in the hospital in a mysterious coma."

"I think I'd better get home and put a few minds at rest."

"I ought to go home too. My mother was in a state when I left."

"But you'll be at school tomorrow?"

"Yes. I don't see why not."

"See you then."

They touched hands briefly.

"See you."

Sixteen

Stephen arrived home to an empty house, which on the whole pleased him. He ran himself a hot bath, completely emptying the tank, and soaked himself with water up to his chin for nearly half an hour. Downstairs again, he hunted through the fridge and kitchen cupboards until he had the ingredients for a large Spanish omelette, which he proceeded to cook slowly and with great care. He was washing it down with a large mug of coffee when Margaret returned home.

"Some cook-up," she said. "I could smell it right down the road." She looked in the fridge. "You are a pig. You've taken all the eggs."

"There were only four."

"Only!"

"There's plenty of cheese."

Margaret picked up the mug of coffee and took a couple of mouthfuls. "I'm going to change," she said and went out again.

But halfway up the stairs she turned and ran back again. "Here! You're supposed to be in the hospital. What happened?"

"Nothing really." Stephen considered telling the whole story but decided against it. "I woke up. That's all there is to it."

"Do you feel all right?"

"Fine."

"The doctor thought you were on a trip."

"He what?"

"Thought you might be under the influence of some drug or other. He didn't say which. But he kept on asking questions."

"You told him I wasn't?"

"Not exactly."

"What is that supposed to mean?"

"Well, we don't know what you are up to, do we? I said that as far as I knew you never had anything to do with that scene. I couldn't be sure, could I?"

"I suppose not. Anyway, it doesn't matter."

"It was that story in the local paper, I expect. Everybody's got drugs on the brain this week."

"What story?"

"See the paper for yourself." She looked around. "I expect it's in the other room; I'll fetch it."

She went through into the lounge and came back almost immediately with the paper. Stephen started to read the account but threw it down after only the first paragraph.

"You're all of a twitch," Margaret said. "Can't you settle somewhere? I've got five chapters of *Redgauntlet* to read before tomorrow."

"Sorry," said Stephen, throwing himself full length on the settee.

"Though why we have to read the horrible book at all defeats me."

Stephen didn't answer and Margaret concentrated in silence on her book for the next ten minutes. Then she looked up and said, "Oughtn't you to be working? When do your 'A' level exams start?"

"About three weeks."

"Well, then."

"I might not take them," Stephen said.

"You *what?*"

"I'm thinking of going off somewhere."

"Not like Sopwith and those other two weeds last year! Dropouts in Majorca or somewhere."

"Something like that," Stephen said.

Margaret put her book down. "Well, I certainly can't concentrate on boring old Scott after that," she said. "How long has this been going on?"

"It came to me in a flash," said Stephen with a laugh. "As I lay here. I suddenly thought, what a stupid lot of old rubbish it all is. Exam, careers . . . all that crap."

"I don't know what Dad'll say."

"What's it all for, anyway? So's you can end up with a bigger car, color TV, and two deep-freeze units? Doesn't it make you sick?"

"No," said Margaret. "Not particularly. I'd rather like to have a color TV."

"Oh, don't talk so silly!"

"That's not the point, anyway, is it?" Margaret said huffily. "What about the family? There'll be the most god-awful row."

"Family?" exclaimed Stephen. "You must be joking. Mum going off to a conference the same day as her precious and only son is being carried off to the hospital in a coma. Kate only lives here because she's mean and doesn't want to pay for a flat of her own. Dad stays at school till all hours working and even goes back in on weekends. That leaves just you and me, doesn't it? Let's stop pretending, shall we? I mean, we're not really a family at all, are we?"

"Pretty average, I should have said."

"We're just an odd collection of people who happen to live in the same house."

"But we're used to each other's oddities."

"We don't really care about each other. We're not committed to each other. . . ."

"I like it that way. It's not my nature to go around helping old ladies anway."

"I'm not talking about old ladies. What about Mum? Do any of us read her books? Do we know what she's up to? No, of course we don't. And we don't care. And what's more she doesn't care whether we do or not."

"I don't know how you can possibly say that. . . ."

"Sticks out a mile. . . ."

"What about Mum? Do you think we ought to send her a telegram or something? To say you're all right?"

"I don't see why."

"But she won't be back for another week."

"That'll be soon enough."

139

"You could be right. We'll leave it to Kate, anyway. She's senior. Let her do the thinking. I'm going to have a bath."

Stephen sat and brooded for a while; then, on an impulse, he went out for a walk. He went down the hill and some distance along the road to town. When he was opposite the old wharf ruins he left the road and went right down onto the bank of the river. From there he could see the gaping entrance to the old warehouse building as a dark, featureless opening. He squatted down on his heels and stared fixedly at the dark shape for about ten minutes, waiting for something but not sure what. In that time he twice thought he saw movement, but it was too brief and undefined for him to decide what was moving.

In the end he stood up stiffly, stretched, and in a vaguely unsettled mood went back to the house.

Seventeen

Next morning at school Stephen felt that Mary was avoiding him, or at least avoiding opportunities for them to talk alone. At break time she disappeared. At lunchtime he was the prefect on duty with the job of prowling the corridors and classrooms, and although he kept a sharp lookout he did not see her anywhere.

About ten minutes before the begining of afternoon school he happened to pass the door of the library and saw that she was there. So, of course, were a number of sixth-formers, having, for the most part, a noisy discussion around the table. Mary was sitting by herself, hugging a radiator by the far window with an open book on her knees.

He stood for a few moments, trying to make up his mind, and then opened the door and walked across to her. She looked up but did not immediately speak.

"I have the feeling," he said slowly, "that you're being somewhat . . . remote. . . ."

"Remote?" Her voice seemed to come from a long

way back. "I had a bad night. I was thinking about what you said yesterday, about being certain. And I'm frightened."

He felt suddenly too self-conscious to press the matter any further. "What are you reading?" he said in a conversational, slightly bantering tone.

" 'The Lady of Shalott.' Do you remember it?"

"Vaguely. We did it for 'O' level."

"I know, but . . . I don't think it registered then. Just so many lines to be quoted . . . 'trailed by slow horses' and so on. But what actually happens . . . it's very odd. It really is. And slightly unnerving. She sits there weaving and watching the real world through a mirror."

"That's right. I remember. And then Sir Lancelot comes jingling along looking like the answer to every maiden's prayer and, bingo, the mirror cracks from side to side."

"But why does it crack?"

"A sort of cosmic warning to the lady that she can't have him."

"Is that why your windshield cracked?"

"Well, windshields do crack, you know."

"So do mirrors. No, I think the mirror cracked because the lady wanted to pass through it. She and Sir Lancelot are in two different worlds."

"And when she insisted on going through, it killed her."

"Well, of course. No one can live in two worlds at the same time. Where were you when part of you was lying around in a coma?"

"I told you."

"I know. And you met yourself—like the mirror cracking, wasn't it?"

The bell rang for afternoon sessions. The group at the table dispersed. Mary stood up and went over to the shelf to replace the Tennyson.

"Have you got a library period today?" Stephen asked.

"Yes. Third period this afternoon."

"I've got phys. ed. I'll skip it and come up here. Unless you want to work."

"No. There's something I want to tell you. Yesterday I wasn't sure. Now I think I am."

"See you."

Eighteen

When Stephen got back to the library it was empty. He stared out of the window for a while, stroking the ridges of the radiator with his fingertips and letting his thoughts take their own disorganized way. Then he remembered what Mary had been saying about the Shalott poem and he went over toward the poetry shelves. But before he reached them he stopped, for no reason that he could identify, to look at one of the group photographs that hung above the shelves all around the library. These photographs were a traditional, and mainly disregarded, decoration. Each one was a group of the prefects for the year, and since the school had been in existence for eighteen years there were eighteen of these groups.

When Mary came into the library a few minutes later she found Stephen standing in front of one of these photographs.

"Come over here," he said. "Who is that girl?"

"That girl? Don't you remember? We were in the first year then. I thought that lot were awfully grand, didn't you?"

"Do you remember her name?"

"Of course. It's Betty Arcoll. And oddly enough, when I was in the library the other day . . ."

"Betty! I had a sort of crush on her. I'd forgotten all about that. She was in this dream. Only she was called Bitta, which is much the same thing, I suppose."

"It's also my name," said Mary.

"But you're Mary Edna Jacqueline. I saw it on the exam list."

Mary reached for a dictionary from the shelf and after a moment handed it to him open. "There!" she said, pointing.

"Mary," he read. "Bitter. The sea. Latin: *mare*. Also, from Hebrew, Miriam . . . but of course. I knew that. . . ."

"It's like rushing up and down the stairs of a tall building trying to catch the elevator—which is always on another floor."

"What is?"

"This is. We keep being on different levels. You're thinking about Betty Arcoll, idealized as Bitta, which might also be me, only in some other form. And I'm thinking of Betty Arcoll, who works in the public library and saw the same picture that I saw on the microfilm machine."

The library door burst open and they turned to see Streeter standing there in gym clothes.

"Sorry," he said. "Have I interrupted an intimate moment?"

Only then did they realize that they were standing in the middle of the library clasping hands.

"Yes," said Stephen. "You did. So buzz off."

"I bear a message," said Streeter, "which I will first deliver. Mr. Warden would like you, at your earliest convenience, of course, to explain your unannounced absence from phys. ed."

"I don't know about explanations," Stephen said. "I might put my mind to fabricating an excuse."

"Warden is a simple soul; he wouldn't notice a difference." Streeter went on standing at the open door, looking at them with an infuriatingly benign expression on his face.

Mary and Stephen stared at him, pointedly waiting for him to go.

"Heigh-ho," said Streeter. "I was just recalling my own innocent youth—trailing clouds of glory. I repeat, heigh-ho."

Failing to provoke them, Streeter raised two fingers and with a suitably episcopal expression traced an aerial cross. "Bless you, my children," he said. "Go forth and subdivide." With which he left them, closing the door behind him.

Stephen said, "If we went down to the mill—the old wharf—I've got a feeling that everything would come clear."

"Now?"

"I can't think of anything more important to do at this moment."

146

"Not even explaining to Mr. Warden?"

"You have to be joking."

Mary thought a moment. "If we go out through that gap behind the swimming pool we shan't be making ourselves so obvious."

"So obviously together?"

"You know I didn't mean that. But it's so undignified to be hauled back and questioned."

"Right. Behind the changing sheds in five minutes—okay?"

They left the school without being seen and about twenty minutes later were walking along the old towpath. There seemed to be some sort of angling competition going on, for every twenty or thirty paces they had to detour around anglers on camp stools surrounded by their little islands of equipment. This went on as far as the old wharf itself, and there in the middle of the empty courtyard or wharfside a small group of men was walking up and down in front of a long trestle table spread with the papers and paraphernalia of judging.

Stephen and Mary stopped, a little dismayed at this occupation in force of what they had thought of as an essentially lonely spot.

"Will it make any difference?" Mary said.

Stephen looked at the old decayed warehouse yawning blackly in the background.

"I don't see how it can," he said at last. "Anyway, they don't own the place. Let's just wander over there."

Mary seemed to hesitate and he put his arm firmly around her shoulders. "You're frightened?"

"Not really. You seem to know more about it than I do."

"But I met you through there. I swear I did."

"If I can't remember . . . in some way remembering is part of one's identity, isn't it? If I can't remember, then perhaps the person you met wasn't real."

"She was real enough."

"Well . . ."

She slowly put her arm around his waist and they walked in step together toward the ruined opening. Within a few paces of the blackness, Stephen brought them both to a halt. "Now," he said. "What can you see?"

For a few seconds Mary saw nothing; then the darkness seemed to be shifting, moving like stained smoke. "Oh, yes," she breathed. "It's the inside of a room. A long table, scrubbed and white, and a sort of dresser, and . . . is that what you can see?"

"Yes. Go on."

"That white table. You know I scrubbed it and put it out in the yard to bleach in the sun. And that only seems two or three days ago."

Stephen saw that she was trembling and tightened his arm firmly around her shoulder. "Are you still frightened?"

"No. Excited, I think."

"And there's nothing here you would want to come back for? Nothing and nobody?"

"Nothing and nobody. Is it the same for you?"

"Exactly the same."

"What about the other you? The double you met?"

"There can't be two of us, if I'm sure," Stephen said.

"And what about memories? What do you think we carry with us?"

"I don't know. We'll travel light. Then we'll be ready to take over what's already there for us."

She turned and smiled into his face. "What are we waiting for?" she said.

Stephen laughed aloud; she looked so radiant. "In we go, then," he cried.

"I shouldn't, if I were you," said a voice behind them and they spun around to find one of the angling judges standing quite near and looking at them in a kindly but warning way. "It's not safe, you know. Just look at the stones up there in the arch. Ready to drop, I'd say. You go poking around in there and you might fetch the whole lot down on your heads."

He stood there, a short, middle-aged man in raincoat and rubber boots, his hands thrust deep into his pockets, emphasizing his doubts with short nods. "Been there a long time, you know. The council ought to do something about it. Either it's a historic monument or it's a hazard to life and limb. That's the trouble with the council—hates making up its stupid collective mind."

They both realized that they could hardly carry out their plan while this man stood there.

"Well, thanks," Stephen said. "But we weren't going to do anything daft."

The man nodded and turned away. "That's good, then," he said. "I've got kids of my own, you know. Bit older than you."

They waited, smiling, as he wandered back to his

companions by the table. One or two of them turned to look as they were told about the danger of these old ruins, but after a minute or so they lost interest and went back to their task of supervising the fishing contest.

"Now?" whispered Stephen, pressing Mary's arm.

"You're sure we'll still be together on the other side?"

Stephen looked startled as if the thought had not occurred to him. "That's important, isn't it?"

"Very important."

He considered this. "Yes," he said at last. "I am sure."

"All right, then."

They went through the arch together and the blackness swallowed them utterly.

"Those kids went in after all, then," one of the anglers commented cynically.

The man who had spoken to Stephen and Mary looked annoyed. "Well, you can't do more than tell people. Are you sure they went in?"

"First they were standing there and then when I looked next they'd gone."

The man walked over to the opening and cautiously leaned forward so that he could peer around in the darkness. "No one there," he said.

"I could have sworn they went through."

"Well, they're not there now."

He walked away and he had only taken half a dozen steps when there was a loud *crack*. He spun around in time to see the whole of the front of the building collapse in a heap of rubble.

"My God! I had my neck under there a moment ago!"

As the dust cleared, all the men went over and stood

on the edge of the mess and peered into the now exposed back of the building.

"You're sure they weren't in there?"

"Certain. They've gone off somewhere. They're safe enough, I reckon."

Format by Kohar Alexanian
Set in 11 pt. Baskerville
Composed, printed and bound by American Book–Stratford Press, Inc.
HARPER & ROW, PUBLISHERS, INCORPORATED

FEI